GARROW'S BASIN

A GOD KILLERS STORY

SEAN D GREGORY

Also By Sean D Gregory

The God Killers Trilogy

- The Growing Darkness
- Darkness Blooms (June 2025)

GARROW'S BASIN

A GOD KILLERS STORY

Written By:
Sean D Gregory

SeaJay SPS

Pittsburgh

Cover Art By: Sean D Gregory

Illustrations By: Serena Dunlap

Edited by:
RB Michaels & Laura Thompson
Writer's Journey Services

First Edition Printed 2025

For more information, visit:
www.sean-gregory.com

DEDICATION

To the fans that said:

"What the fuck happened to Tamrin and Jesmir?"

I always intended to tell you.

Now you know.

THE SPLIT

Shen led the way down the servants' stairs at the back of the Jester's Pot Inn. Tamrin took up the rear guard, the royal twins and their new Emissary, Krin, safely nestled in the middle. Deliveries and staff danced in delicate side-steps around one another, busy with their part in the transition of the inn from old guests to new. The diverse foot traffic hid the escape of the five-member party as they worked their way into the service alley.

Tamrin, grateful for the cover provided by the organized chaos of activity through the back door, risked a backward glance down the hall. He was relieved to see they hadn't yet been discovered by Brogen or his mercenaries.

The group wasted no time with solemn goodbyes. Brogen had already entered the inn through the front door. Time had run out faster than they expected. At least the prince and princess had time to don disguises.

Tamrin had no clue whether Brogen actually knew that the twin royals stayed at the Inn, but his appearance was hardly a coincidence. Even if he'd selected the Inn by happenstance, the risk that the desk clerk might reveal the presence of Teshket royals to Brogen was too significant. They'd barely had time to gather their things when Shen witnessed Brogen cross Swill Street.

Tamrin turned to Shen, and the two friends clasped arms, neither happy to see the other go.

Filled with a sense of dread, Tamrin smiled at the vagabond vigilante, who was the most crucial person in the world to him. Shen, never one for long lingering farewells, simply nodded in his usual succinct manner.

"Tomorrow night," Shen said. "See you there. Hurry. And stay away from Garrow's Basin."

"That's the plan," Tamrin replied.

For Tamrin, the exchange felt permanent. Then again, it always felt permanent when he left the company of his best friend. The big hunter lived in a perpetual state of worry, brought on by the fear that Shen's propensity for self-harm meant every departure could be the last. The thought that Shen would do something rash was the only genuine fear that Tamrin couldn't overcome in this world.

He swallowed hard, pushed his fears aside, and propelled the prince down the alley. Charged with protecting his half of the royal sibling pair, Tamrin was eager to get the hell out of Valshannon and reconnect with Shen,

Jesma, and Krin in Rogue's Pointe two days hence. Prince Jesmir, distraught over his separation from his twin sister Jesma, resisted Tamrin's instructions at first. But Tamrin's calm insistence and immovable presence forced the prince to comply. The pair headed down the dank alley, opposite the direction of the other three members of their party, without another word.

Tamrin's separation anxiety triggered immediate heart palpitations. As he left Shen behind to take a different path out of Valshannon, he fought back the misty-eyed emotion that threatened to distract him from his task. He imagined Shen with his usual "do as I say" attitude in full effect as the infamous vigilante hurried the princess and her Emissary through the Valshannon streets toward the northwest gate. He allowed the imaginary picture of Shen's receding form to linger for a moment longer before he wrestled his thoughts into submission.

Tamrin and Prince Jesmir slipped through the throng of the servants' alley traffic and did their best to blend in.

"We need to move fast," Tamrin said to the prince over the din of carts, footsteps, dropped crates, and chatter.

Tamrin was relieved that Jesmir's appearance no longer drew attention the way it had the night before. They'd dyed silver hair black. With a wardrobe change from torn royal garb to that of modest merchant clothing, the prince was disguised enough, at least at a glance, to blend in.

As long as nobody looked too closely, they stood a chance to get away unaccosted. Jesmir helped their cause by keeping his gaze low, his bright blue eyes and pale white skin a dead giveaway that would raise suspicions.

———

Jesmir dealt with his own anxieties as he marched down the alley with reluctant resignation. He couldn't suppress the fear that he'd just seen his sister for the last time. Their abrupt separation heightened his sorrow, the threat of the loss of his sister compounding the recent loss of his father. Too much was left unsaid, but there was little time to say it. Instead, he obediently rushed through the crowd, desperate to end this part of their journey and reunite with his twin. He should have at least told her he loved her. She was all he had left of his family. He wanted her to know how much she meant to him.

The twins had been through much together in recent weeks. Kidnapped from their ship by pirates, they'd escaped their captors and somehow managed to survive the leap off the cliff into the Brine River. Against all odds, they'd evaded Brogen and his mercenaries and escaped Killinshire, the homeland of their bitter enemy. Together, they braved the RhineWoods of Rhinestab, inarguably the most dangerous region of the Five Realms.

They breathed a sigh of relief when they reached Winding Run. For the briefest moment, they thought they were home free. They were halfway home and in the land of their closest allies.

But the gods were cruel, and the twins were besieged by bandits. Jesmir fought as best he could, but there were four of them and only one of him. The sibling's luck had finally run out.

Or so they thought.

Jesmir didn't harbor any delusions of grandeur over his prowess in combat. He was not a warrior. His intellect and skill focused more on people and the business of helping…or wooing. If not for the timely appearance of Shen, he and his sister would both be dead, or worse, and Jesmir knew it.

But Shen *had* shown up, followed not shortly thereafter by Tamrin. The same Tamrin who now pushed the prince through the crowded alley.

Jesmir marveled at how the two strangers risked their own safety to protect the prince and princess from harm. He had no clue why they did what they did, but he was grateful. He barely knew these new travel companions, yet he trusted them. He trusted them more than he trusted himself.

Desperation requires desperate acts, he thought.

It was no slight risk to trust the strange duo. But the enigmatic Shen, readily violent and filled with sarcasm, twice came to their rescue. He asked for nothing in return. He'd even left behind the bandits' money to aid in the lost royals' return home. Without any fanfare, he simply vanished back from whence he came.

They never expected to see their rescuer again.

Injured, tired, and frightened, they fled the scene of the attack, only to run into more trouble at the banks of the Great Rankin River. Once again, the mysterious Shen appeared, ready to rescue. Jesmir sensed that Shen somehow felt responsible for their safe return home and harbored some guilt over leaving them after his valiant rescue the day before.

Still, even that incredible act of service wasn't enough for Jesmir to fully trust the two men.

It wasn't until he overheard last night's conversation between them, a conversation they only felt safe to take part in because they believed Jesmir had fallen asleep, that Jesmir understood. The two men spoke in earnest as Tamrin confronted Shen with suspicion. Jesmir nearly gasped when Tamrin said that he knew Shen was the infamous Harbinger. With that revelation, the events of the previous two days fell into perspective.

The man who rescued them and now escorted Jesma on her path home was the Harbinger. Everyone in the Five Realms had heard of the infamous vigilante. No one knew his true identity. The legend of The Harbinger of Death had resulted in the largest bounty ever placed in the Five Realms—a bounty that grew almost daily and had existed for three decades.

To the ordinary people, the Harbinger was a known protector of those in need. To villains like Captain Brogen of the Dark Guard, he was a bane, a threat to their power and titles.

Many believed the Harbinger to be a ghost or a collective of many different vigilantes disguising themselves behind a singular persona—a myth meant to draw everyone off the scent. Even the most blessed of the Great Eight had failed to bring the vigilante to justice. But now Jesmir knew the truth, and in that knowledge rested the hope of Jesma's safe return. Jesma couldn't be in better hands—at least in theory.

Unfortunately, Jesmir recognized a fatal flaw in the Harbinger. Shen was reckless and quite possibly incapable of avoiding risk. It was almost as if the vigilante was addicted to the rush of danger…or had a death wish. Jesmir couldn't discern which was more accurate. Still, neither option was reassuring, and he found himself worried maybe Jesma wasn't as safe as he wanted to believe. Jesmir's head spun as he seesawed between relief and worry.

Still, the best trackers and assassins sought the Harbinger. Yet, thirty years later, the Harbinger still lived. Jesmir allowed himself to have faith that Shen would see to Jesma's safety. He had no real reason to think otherwise.

That left the prince with Tamrin, a man who had been hired by Brogen to track down the royal twins. If not for Shen's timely arrival once again, Tamrin would not have learned the truth in time to prevent a disheartening end to the twins' plight. Shen's intercession and relationship with Tamrin stopped the tracker from handing the siblings back to Brogen.

Again, the Harbinger arrives just in time, Jesmir thought.

He wondered if they were all simple pawns in some greater plot by the gods. So many unanswered prayers left him with little doubt about his personal unimportance in their schemes. A lifetime of ignored pleas and supplications to the Great Eight left Jesmir with a crisis of faith. Weeks on the run had further eroded his trust that even one of the gods cared about him. The constant doubt tore into his psyche left him in a spiritual abyss.

Unanswered prayers plagued him. Even in his desperation, no god granted him access to magic. His sister and mother were blessed by Ezra, and his father by Shamna. But Jesmir felt no favor extended his way by any of his patrons, though he prayed to them all.

Jesmir forced himself to focus on the now. With deliberate intent, he placed one foot in front of the other, marching further away from his last tie to his previous life. He knew the internal lamentations that grew with the distance between him and his sister weren't healthy or helpful. But he couldn't shake his tortured thoughts. Deep down, he knew why, and the truth hit him hard.

He'd reached the limit of himself, and the gods found him lacking. They didn't grant him powers like the rest of his family because they couldn't see in him what they saw in Jesma. He was not special. He was not worthy. He brought no value to the table.

The beleaguered prince was dangerously close to his breaking point.

At least he and his sister no longer had to navigate the long trip home alone. If he was honest, he was happy to relinquish the responsibility of decisions.

He knew enough from his studies and the lessons of the last few days to know that more trouble lay ahead than behind. There were only two paths through the Toerge Mountains that formed the border between Rhinestab, his home realm of Teshket—at least as far as he was aware. One of which Brogen was certain to assume as their likely route. Their pursuer would hurry toward ValleyView in an effort to intercept his prey. Brogen would never suspect the other choice was an option. Jesmir had no clue what Shen's plan was once they reunited at Rogue's Pointe, but he hoped it wasn't that other option…Jesmir didn't even want to think about the other option.

They had over two hundred miles left to reach home. What remained of their journey was fraught with threats he'd only ever imagined: spiderlyches, the Cuska, Raysons, not to mention the Picaroons. Every danger ahead was more adept at survival in the wild than he was. That worry alone was sufficient for the day. The RhineWoods had a reputation, one he'd already discovered was well deserved. And he was only half-way through the cursed lands.

At least they'd successfully located their emissary, as protocol required. The arrival of the queen's emissary this morning increased their odds of survival. He'd always wondered why the protocol was necessary. As kids, he and his sister never took it seriously. But they'd been obedient in the practice. Now, he was glad they had.

The Emissary.

Jesmir's thoughts drifted to the strange, scarred woman who had arrived earlier today. She wasn't what Jesmir expected. There was a fierce hardness to her, much like Shen. Instead of the refined presence of a dignitary, she was gruff, rougher around the edges—less like him or his sister and more like Shen and Tamrin. She was forceful, like the feral vigilante.

Jesmir considered the exchange between Emissary Krin and the Harbinger. The two interacted with guarded dialogue—the type of communication that indicated a hidden history.

Had the others noticed the tension between the two? he wondered.

The Emissary seemed displeased with Shen's unwillingness to concede to her authority. The tension Jesmir witnessed could have been a simple turf war–two dominant personalities vying for their position as leader. An emissary of the queen wouldn't be too happy with a ragged threadbare, nobody usurping her authority. That could explain the tension he observed.

No, Jesmir thought, *That's not it.*

The prince navigated social queues with the same skill as Tamrin tracked his prey. The two—vigilante and Emissary—spoke with an intimate knowledge of how the other would react. There was more to the exchange between Emissary Krin and Shen than what appeared on the surface. They had familiarity.

They knew one another before today. Jesmir was sure of it. Jesmir hoped whatever history the two shared wouldn't cause problems for his sister.

Jesmir glanced back, hoping for one final glimpse of his sister. Instead, Tamrin smiled a meager smile as he prodded the prince forward. Jesmir saw the big man's reluctance as well.

Jesmir smiled back at the giant monstrosity of a man. Tamrin's genuine kindness and gentle reassurance seemed rooted in an inherent interest for the well-being of others. The hairy, heavily bearded man had shown more compassion in any singular moment than Jesmir had experienced in the entirety of his escape from Brogen's men in Killinshire.

Tamrin nudged the Prince in the shoulder, forcing Jesmir to pick up the pace. Like it or not, Jesmir understood that his best chance of survival was to do as he was instructed, so he accepted the inappropriate handling with only a mild grumble of protest.

He understood what Tamrin needed from him. His real objection to all of this centered on his anxiety over leaving his sister.

If she died, he'd be the last of his family. Save the queen, of course.

His thoughts turned to Brogen, and his mind filled with the image of their father as their last surviving parent bled to death on the soil of his sworn enemy.

Damn, Brogen, for this. I swear it will be me who takes your last breath.

RESERVATIONS FOR TWO

The alley opened onto the main street toward the southern gate through which Tamrin and Jesmir entered the night before. Though the exit onto the thoroughfare was less than one hundred yards from the servant's exit of the Jester's Pot Inn, it took several minutes to reach the wide-open street. As with the alley, the early morning bustle of citizens, guards, and merchants eager to get their wares into the willing hands of buyers who frequented Swill Street was well underway.

Tamrin's skin tingled along his spine, and he tensed.

Fildeus' blessing of the magic that triggered whenever Tamrin was observed without his knowledge was his most prized skill. For a person of Tamrin's size, unable to hide effectively, the spell was a lifesaver on more than one occasion. Passive and non-violent, the skill gave him the greatest chance to avoid needless confrontations.

Nearly a full head taller than the next tallest member of the mid-morning crowd, there was little chance the monstrous man could blend in outside of his home village in Haabrestand, where Tamrin was considered average build. Dressed as he was in his collection of furs amongst the wealthy city of Valshannon, Tamrin couldn't stand out more if he tried. He kept his head lowered—a futile effort to keep curious eyes off him. Tamrin's long dark beard, tied off at the end with his stone periapt of faith, braided long hair, and large war hammer strapped across his back were impossible to hide.

If Fildeus hadn't seen fit to reward her favored hunter with the spell that gave him information, Tamrin would never have escaped anywhere. This time, the spell informed Tamrin that someone in the alley behind him had watched his flight from the Inn. That was a bad omen.

The tingle on his skin forced him to accelerate through the crowd, an action that caused the prince to stutter-step in response, the smaller man's feet already moving at an uncomfortable pace. The vibrating sensation traveled across Tamrin's back, and he knew whoever watched moved through the crowd behind him, just as he and Jesmir shifted through the crowd.

Jesmir sulked as his legs fought to maintain the brisk pace without breaking into a conspicuous jog. Tamrin sensed the prince's displeasure with his current predicament, but there was no time for niceties. He felt horrible for the disrespect he extended toward his royal charge. He didn't relish the gruffness the situation called for, but the prince's life was in his hands. Shen had tasked him to keep the prince safe. Tamrin would do whatever it took, even if it violated his own personal nature.

Tough hands were required at this moment, and though the young royal had been through one hell of an ordeal the last few weeks, their enemy was hot on their tracks. Tamrin empathized with the younger man's state of mind. Separating him from his twin sister didn't go without a fight, but Shen was adamant. And, as usual, Shen got his way.

The signals that tingled Tamrin's body grew more intense, and his nerves ached. The danger was too close for comfort. He hoped like hell it wasn't Brogen himself that followed them. If it was Brogen, or Brogen's mercenaries, there would be no talking his way out of his betrayal. Tamrin violated his original contract, opting to rescue the very man Brogen had hired him to apprehend.

He positioned his tall, bulky frame right behind Jesmir and hoped his body offered an effective visual screen. With a gentle but firm grip, he steered Jesmir by the shoulder and propelled the prince forward. Jesmir startled at the touch and then responded with faster footsteps. The duo couldn't lag any longer. They broke into a slight jog, unperturbed by the angry glances from those they pushed aside. There was no more time for formalities. His grip on the royal shoulder tightened. It carried a command.

Move your ass.

Tamrin's heartbeat accelerated. The suspicion that their tail was Brogen sent a different shiver up Tamrin's spine. One not born of magic but of fright. No one was ever known to survive an encounter with the Captain of The Dark Guard. Tamrin would face off with the man if necessary. But if he could avoid it until Shen was nearby, he had every intention of doing just that.

Brogen was *the* killer among a nation of killers. The realm of Killinshire, several hundred miles to the south, didn't breed compassionate people the way Haabrestand, Tamrin's home realm, did. And Brogen was the worst of them all. Tamrin wasn't even sure Shen could beat that man, and no one was better than Shen.

Tamrin scanned the street on their way, hoping for another horse-drawn taxi like the one they'd found on their entry into the sprawling city the night before. But he couldn't risk reliance on hope. Hope was for fools who failed to act on their own volition. Still, he offered a silent prayer to Fildeus, his hand on the periapt of his patron tied into his beard for emphasis.

The tracker and prince forced their way through the crowd to put as much distance between themselves and the Jester's Pot Inn as possible. If Shen was right, and his friend usually was, their pursuers would discover that the lot of them had checked in last night. It was only a matter of time before they realized their quarry had only just slipped away.

The growing tingle on his spine attested that they might have already been discovered.

Why did I have to order that breakfast? He thought.

Shamna be praised if they could roll the lucky twenty-three and escape Valshannon unimpeded by Brogen's mercenaries.

Tamrin's right shoulder and arm began to tingle. Another set of eyes located them. Tamrin dared not look back for fear of revealing his intentions. He'd betrayed the contract, but Brogen's mercenaries didn't know it yet. If he was lucky, they thought Tamrin chased someone. As long as Tamrin kept the prince screened from view, he could hold on to the ruse that he was just a tracker in pursuit.

Brogen's thugs would discover the truth soon enough. It didn't have to be right now.

Tamrin's pride still stung from the way he'd fallen for Brogen's lies. Had he realized who his employer was, he would never have taken the job.

Thank Fildeus, I ran into Shen, he thought.

"We've gotta get out of here," he mumbled to himself, the deep baritone of his voice startling a young woman who passed in the other direction. He mumbled an apology and continued to shove the prince forward. Tamrin scanned the crowd ahead. His skin scanned the path behind.

It's up to me to keep you safe, Your Highness, he thought.

Tamrin's thoughts returned to Shen. Tamrin hated that they weren't together. He desired to keep his friend close, safe from his inner demons. These demons threatened to overwhelm the depressed former assassin.

I just love the little guy so damn much, Tamrin thought.

Tamrin always worried about Shen, but he was more worried now. The glaze in his best friend's eyes had returned. He fought back a twinge of panic when he thought about Shen's propensity for self-harm.

Tamrin missed his friend every second they weren't together. He couldn't contain his excitement when Shen actually appeared at his own birthday celebration two days prior. He'd expected Shen not to show. Tamrin was accustomed to the fear, but it never got easier. He lived within the delicate space between hope and worry. It was the one true constant of his relationship with Shen. That and his unrequited love.

Tamrin lived in a pervasive state of expectant disappointment and eternal hope. Somehow, the gods always interceded before Shen could succeed in any suicide plan.

Thank you, Fildeus, for interceding on my behalf, Tamrin prayed. *Even if Shen thinks prayers don't work.*

Tamrin knew that his fears were unfounded this time. The only reason he even agreed to the current plan was that Shen was a man of commitment. Shen promised to get the twin royals home safely. Shen never failed to deliver on his promises. Tamrin held on to that assurance and put his worries aside. He knew, this time, he would see his friend again.

Tamrin had tried so many times to get Shen to promise not to take his own life. But Shen always refused to make such a promise.

"I long ago accepted that I would die by my own hand," Shen said far too often.

Tamrin feared nothing more in the world than the day Shen was gone. Tears welled up in his eyes at the thought.

He choked them back and wrestled his focus to their flight from Valshannon and the effort to evade Captain Brogen. The prince stumbled before him, and Tamrin caught him before the man went down. Folks parted slightly, caught by surprise.

Tamrin felt sorry for the young royal, whose safety was now his responsibility. The prince was ill-prepared for his recent troubles. They'd escaped from Killinshire into Rhinestab only to suffer a near-fatal attack by bandits, nearly drowned in the Great Rankin River by Grankin, the God of Time, and now were separated for the first time in their weeks-long ordeal. It was a lot for anyone to experience. But the prince, accustomed to a life of ease, suffered from trauma build-up. Tamrin wasn't sure how much more the man could take.

A familiar orange hat with three large purple feathers appeared before them. The hat rested on the head of a man perched atop a black carriage. Tamrin steered Jesmir through the crowd. A sigh of relief escaped his lips. The cabbie looked down and smiled as they approached.

"Twice in two days," the man said, his broad, toothless grin at once eager and welcoming. "Where are the rest of your group?"

"We are racing them to Winding Run. How quickly can you get us to the south gate?" Tamrin asked, breathless.

"How fast you need?"

"Yesterday. It's a race."

The cabby laughed. "Two copper and I can get you there in three minutes. Three copper, I'll get ya there in two and won't stop for the authorities," the cabbie said with a chuckle.

"Sold for three copper," Tamrin replied and pushed the Prince toward the step ladder.

Tamrin climbed aboard the carriage and dropped two pieces of copper into the cabbie's open palm. He plopped down next to Jesmir.

"You'll get the third if you can make it in two minutes. Keep your face down," Tamrin whispered.

The cabby laughed. The prince, his face a frozen mask of fear, nodded and ducked down below the carriage wall.

"Let's go," Tamrin instructed the cabbie.

With a sudden jerk that threw Tamrin backward into the seat, the cab accelerated. It wasn't until he leaned back that he realized the tingles in his skin diminished. He could still feel the magic burn inside him, so he knew the magic was still active. Whoever had eyes on them had finally lost sight.

STOUTHEARTED PRINCE

The cabbie brought the carriage to a stop outside the southern gates of Valshannon. True to his word, he'd made excellent time and managed to reach the gates before the Goddess of Light fully ascended over the treetops. Both sides of the King's Regal Highway teemed with vendors amid their morning opening rituals. Wooden shutters on semi-permanent stands creaked as they opened. Farmers set up their carts tied to mules and arranged their produce. Guards eyed everyone with mild suspicion.

Ezra's rays illuminated the sky from the horizon in brilliant ribbons of color—bright reds, pinks, and yellow streaks pierced wispy clouds with beams that spread wider as they approached overhead. Her blazing body, still partially hidden behind the tall trees of the RhineWoods, slowly rose ever higher into the sky. In the distance, the shade of the trees held King's Regal Highway in the cool morning darkness, its southward trail disappearing in the shade ahead.

"Thank you," Tamrin said to the cabbie, who nodded in reply.

Tamrin nudged the prince out of the carriage and pointed east. The Prince stood and watched the activity along the highway. They stepped off the carriage, and the cabbie tipped his orange hat, feathers flowing in the light breeze. Tamrin handed the cabby a third copper and watched the horse-drawn carriage turn back under the grand southern gates of Valshannon.

The two men left the packed dirt highway, Prince Jesmir in front, and followed a well-worn eastward path that ran the outer perimeter of Valshannon's massive stone walls.

Frequented by travelers with a desire to avoid the busy streets within the walls of the great city, the wide trail was clear of foliage but unkempt—muddy and bumpy in the low spots. Bordered on one side by the great stone wall and on the other by the giant oaks and maples of the RhineWoods, the trail followed the curve of the massive city's defensive border.

Tamrin and Jesmir followed the trail for over a mile, still in a hurry. Jesmir focused on the construction of the wall that protected Valshannon from invasion for thousands of years. Lost in his thoughts, he walked, shoulders slumped, eyes intent on the smooth stone structure. He wondered how, after so much time, the walls remained smooth, pristine, and untouched by time.

Tamrin resumed his task of protector and kept his eyes in constant motion, his attention divided between the prince's safety and their route. He remained watchful for the trailhead that signaled their entrance into the RhineWoods that would send them straight toward Garrow's Basin.

He wished again for Shen's presence. As much as they needed to exit Valshannon, they needed to navigate Garrow's Basin with haste. If Shen had been present, they might have braved the direct route through Garrow's Basin and cut a half-day from the trip. But without the most feared fighter on the continent in their ranks, Tamrin felt it was best to avoid Rayson territory. Shen had a history with the Raysons that Tamrin, on his own, could not take advantage of.

He certainly couldn't risk the life of his charge in an attempt to negotiate safe passage through the Raysons' home territory.

Tamrin felt no shame in his admission that he was terrified of the Raysons. He had no desire to deal with them ever, especially not today. The strange clan kept a stranglehold on the territory that even the King of Rhinestab couldn't break. Moreover, the Raysons had no love for trespassers. The residents of Garrow's Basin held strange powers and were believed to suffer from centuries of intense inbreeding. Tamrin wasn't even sure they were human.

Or living.

Tempting them was never a good idea. The Rayons are one of the more feared dangers in Conishant. Tamrin could take care of himself in most situations, but when it came to the Raysons, he had little confidence he could survive alone. And even with the present company, against the Raysons, he was alone. Tamrin was certain that if the worst happened, the prince would prove more liability than an asset. Prince Jesmir's sword and short bow appeared as useful in his soft hands as a periapt of faith in the faithless Shen's. He'd never seen the prince fight, but Tamrin knew warriors. Jesmir was no warrior.

"Your Highness, how you holding up?" Tamrin asked in his deep baritone.

The prince didn't respond.

"I need you to communicate, Your Highness," Tamrin said, his tone gentle.

The prince replied, "I should have stayed with my sister."

Tamrin wanted to argue but couldn't. He agreed with the Prince's sentiment and preferred the group stay together as well. But Shen made a valid point. Their pursuers searched for two siblings of identical age, a silver-blond man and a silver-blonde woman with pale skin and blue eyes, dressed in royal attire, who may or may not be with a single escort of unknown description. Disguised and separated, their chances of an undetected escape improved dramatically.

Better still, since neither party held any semblance to those descriptions.

"This was the right choice," Tamrin replied. "We'll meet up with her and the others in Rogue's Pointe by sundown tomorrow. Let's pick up the pace," he said.

The prince offered no acknowledgment to the counterpoint and trudged ahead. He increased his stride, and Tamrin took that as a sign he'd been heard.

Tamrin opened his mouth to say more, but a new tingle in his spine interrupted his thoughts. He slowed his pace and reached out with his magic. The sensation spread across his back again. The discomfort, mild at first, grew more intense with each step. He glanced over his shoulder and inspected the path behind him, this time less concerned with inconspicuous behavior. The trail behind was empty for several hundred yards.

He turned to inspect his surroundings, and the sensation shifted around his body, a search beacon. Somewhere, the observer hid. Tamrin concentrated on the sensation and pinpointed the direction of the lurker. Somewhere in the shadows of the tree line, someone had eyes on them. His cheeks and chest hummed with energy, and Tamrin knew he faced the right direction.

Motion within the shadows of the trees drew his eye and confirmed his suspicion. A dark form darted among the trunks as the intensity of the signal increased. Tamrin pursed his lips.

Definitely hostile. Tamrin turned back to the prince in a slow, easy motion. He couldn't discern who hid in the trees, but he was sure their pursuers had found them.

Tamrin remained calm, and he stepped closer to Jesmir, the magic signals shifting back toward his spine again.

"Your Highness," Tamrin whispered, "step toward the forest line."

"Why?" the prince demanded.

"Please step into the trees," Tamrin said, his tone forceful.

The prince stopped. His attitude was at once belligerent and a bit frightened.

"But why?"

Tamrin bit back a retort. Shen had feared this would happen when traveling with royals on the run. Tamrin should have emphasized the mandate for blind obedience that Shen threw down earlier. But Tamrin's nature was not to demand. Rather than argue, he grabbed the prince, putting a finger to his lips to keep him quiet, and drug him into the woods. They worked their way deeper into the darker shadows, taking an indirect line. Tamrin located a dense spot of shrubbery and tucked the prince behind it.

As expected, his sudden motion triggered their pursuer to rush from their hiding place in the shadows. Tamrin watched as the man was unsure exactly where they had entered the woods.

"Tamrin!" a familiar voice called out.

Tamrin grimaced. He recognized the voice of the man in the shadows. They'd been hired together by the same man Tamrin was now desperate to escape. Tamrin gave Jesmir a stern look and held his palm out to the prince in a signal to stay put. The Prince finally understood and responded with a curt nod, his face a mask of fear. Tamrin put his finger to his lips again and hoped the prince obeyed his commands. To Tamrin's relief, Jesmir remained silent.

Good, Tamrin thought.

Tamrin grabbed the periapt in his beard and whispered another silent prayer to Fildeus. He stretched out his magic to sense for others in the woods. The extra effort within the magic caused his skin to burn a little hotter, and sweat built on his brow, but he received no indication others lay in wait. Satisfied that only one pursuer existed in the area, he turned his attention to the voice and stepped out toward the speaker. He called out quietly.

"Rooker?"

A tall, thin man with dark hair and eyes turned toward Tamrin, his gaze shifting beyond the giant tracker and into the woods. Tamrin took in the man's appearance with new eyes. Thin, wiry, hard, and with his beard shaped into a pointed goatee, Tamrin realized that he missed all the signs before. Everything about the man screamed, 'Officer in the Killinshire Army.'

Tamrin admonished himself. Shen was right, Tamrin had been duped into the job of tracking the royals. He'd fallen for a simple wardrobe disguise. He made a mental note to be more observant in the future. He should have recognized that the men that hired him in Dresdin were Killinfolk soldiers. Tamrin inherently believed in the good of people, while his best friend believed in the opposite.

"I thought that was you. I've been chasing after you since Swill Street," Rooker said and took a step closer to the big tracker. Tamrin noted that the heel of Rooker's palm rested on the hilt of his sword. The man's eyes shifted around the woods from where Tamrin emerged.

"Where's Kairn?" Rooker asked.

Tamrin shrugged at the reference to the companion he'd left behind in the Great Rankin River yesterday—not long after the man's true intentions were revealed.

"We separated," Tamrin said truthfully. "He went west on one path. I headed east." Another true statement, though vague and pertinent details like 'as a prisoner of the God of Time' were left out.

"But I thought I saw you with someone," Rooker replied.

"Nope, just me," Tamrin lied. He knew Rooker wasn't buying the lie.

Rooker eyed Tamrin with suspicion.

"Where the hell have you been? Brandin's been asking about you. You were supposed to meet us at the Rankin yesterday." The man paused a little too long. "You. And Kairn."

Tamrin flexed his muscles in impatience, time running short.

"Well, Kairn followed the trail west," Tamrin said with a point. "I chose to go home. I'm no longer interested in the job. The Great Rankin River settled the matter. Frankly, this job isn't paying enough to risk encounters with River Gnomes."

Rooker gave Tamrin a look that bordered on disbelief.

"You were paid half in advance," Rooker accused.

Tamrin reached into his purse and pulled out three gold coins.

"Here, give the boss his money back. I quit. Tell Brogen, I mean Brandin…" his words cut short as he realized his mistake.

Nadur's nuts! Tamrin screamed inside.

Tamrin couldn't backstep from what he'd said. Rooker reacted with instant aggression. Fluid and quick, Rooker's sword unsheathed, and its blade swiped at Tamrin's neck. The motion was so quick. If Tamrin hadn't expected an attack, he'd be headless already.

Rooker's action was the final confirmation that Shen was right. Tamrin's employer had ill intent. Rooker stood too close for Tamrin to grab his periapt and pray for more protection from Fildeus. The mercenary closed the remaining gap between them with another sword slash.

Tamrin growled. This fight was up to him, with no help from Fildeus.

"Now that's unfortunate," Rooker said. "Figured out his name wasn't really Brandin, did ya?"

Tamrin stepped back two large paces, hands up, in an effort to get them closer to the stone talisman tied to his beard. "Hey now, watch where you point that thing."

"Who's with you?" Rooker asked, his gaze once again skirting around the big man's wide frame into the woods beyond.

"I told you. Nobody."

Rooker lunged forward with another thrust of his sword. The quick swipe at Tamrin narrowly missed, but the tracker was faster on his feet than his size would show possible.

"My bet is you had a change of heart. Heard the spoiled little brats' sob story about how we killed their father? Which one you got? The sniveling prince? Or the tasty morsel of a princess?"

"I don't know what you're talking about," Tamrin said. Anger rose as he dodged another swipe of the soldier's sword.

"Liar," Rooker snarled. "I'm going to kill you, tracker. Then take your prisoner as my own. I'll be the hero of the day. The captain will probably give me a promotion."

Tamrin took enormous steps back and to the side, his motions deliberate. His long stride forced Rooker to hurry forward to keep up. Tamrin dodged two more sword strikes and saw an opening. He surprised Rooker with a quick step inside the man's attack and spun around the smaller fighter. Tamrin caught the smaller man's arm in his massive hands and snarled. Rooker's face contorted with discomfort from the strength of Tamrin's grip. With a twist of his hips and an explosive grunt, Tamrin tossed his attacker toward the stone city wall, lifting Rooker's two feet from the ground.

To Tamrin's amazement, Rooker recovered quickly and twisted his body midair to land on his feet. The soldier slid along the muddy path on one foot and planted the other against the wall behind him, his eyes still on Tamrin. With the new leverage, Rooker lunged himself forward, the tip of his blade carving a crisscross pattern at Tamrin.

The kind-hearted hunter barely managed to release his war hammer in time. Rooker's blade sliced in a downward arc at Tamrin's head. A loud clang echoed through the trees and reverberated off the city wall. Just in time,

Tamrin's long Korund steel handle blocked the sword's edge.

Tamrin grinned wide, his perfectly straight, perfectly white teeth flashed within his deep, dark facial hair. A twinkle sparked in his eye as he and Rooker pressed close.

"You know," Tamrin said, "I wish my friend could see this. He loves to watch me pummel you, Kill-intwerps."

Rooker's sword flicked with expert strikes but failed to find an opening in Tamrin's defenses. For his size, Tamrin moved with the grace of an animal. Rooker spun on his toes and brought the sword down for another overhead strike. Tamrin's handle caught the blade again. This time, Rooker torqued his wrist sideways with the impact, and the blade fell into a flat position against Tamrin's handle. Rooker drew his sword down, attempting to catch the big man's hand with the sharp edge of his sword.

Sparks flew as the Korund steel blade ground against the Korund steel gnarled handle. Tamrin released his lower hand as he sidestepped the sword's arc. He pressed forward with his body weight and drove Rooker off balance, his teeth exposed in an animalistic snarl. Rooker responded with a dive to the side and tucked himself into a roll several feet away from Tamrin's massive frame. Rooker reversed his core and came up on his feet, ready to strike again, his mouth twisted in fury.

Tamrin's hammer flew along a short, underhanded arc toward Rooker's midsection, the attack much faster than Rooker thought possible. With a look of surprise, Rooker opted to fall backward rather than step inward and avoid the blow entirely. Tamrin, mid-swing, re-angled the path, and his momentum brought the hammer up over his head in a long recovery.

Rooker used the time to press his advantage. Rather than attack again, he pulled out a periapt of Hakaka and chanted a prayer in Killinspeak. Tamrin's eyes grew wide. He realized he was too far away from Rooker to stop the spell. Tamrin reached up to grip his own periapt. His only chance to avoid the spell was a protection prayer. Tamrin hoped Fildeus favored him in this fight with direct attention and that his prayer would be received. His eyes closed in earnest concentration, Tamrin touched the stone within his beard.

Rooker's chant echoed off the wall of Valshannon, "Alth ahn, der chesk...."

The next word was garbled as the prayer stopped mid-chant. Instead of words, Tamrin heard a shocked gasp. He opened one eye, expecting the worst, as he began his counter-prayer.

Tamrin's prayer hung in his throat. He opened the other eye and stared in surprise. Rooker stood, mouth agape, eyes wide. Crimson red spread along Rooker's chest. Tamrin watched as Rooker stumbled forward and fought to stay upright. A metal sword sprouted from the center of the stain, driven from behind. The blade, covered in blood, protruded from Rooker's sternum, its tip pointed directly at Tamrin. Rooker stared down at the metal blade, his eyes wide with horror. He looked up at Tamrin and snarled.

"He'll find them. You can't run forever."

Tamrin shook his head. "Well, maybe, but you won't be able to tell him anything, so I like our chances."

Rooker tried to say more, but his eyes went blank, and he fell forward. His momentum yanked the body of a stunned prince forward from the shadows. Jesmir, eyes wide in horror, released the sword and fought to maintain his balance. As the dead man fell to his knees, his torso flopped forward. The sword wedged into the soft, wet ground, and Rooker fell to rest at an awkward angle, held in a forward lean by the sword.

"Well, Your Highness," Tamrin said with a smile. "Looks like maybe you can use that thing after all."

With a hand on the sword's pommel, Tamrin planted a boot on Rooker's back and yanked the sword free. The soldier's body fell to the ground with a solid thud. Tamrin wiped the blade on Rooker's clothes and flipped the hilt toward Jesmir, who accepted the sword with a shaky hand. Jesmir stared down at Rooker, horrified by what he'd done.

"I... I... I've never killed a man before," he whispered.

Tamrin raised his left eyebrow in response and turned back to the mercenary's body. He watched Rooker's blood pool on the ground beneath him. He set his war hammer back into its harness, squatted down over Rooker, and dipped two fingers into the blood around the hole in Rooker's back. He glanced over his shoulder and waved Jesmir to come closer. Their eyes locked, and the prince finally acknowledged Tamrin.

Tamrin stood. Towering over the prince by more than a foot, Tamrin smiled down at Jesmir.

"What are you doing?"

"You've taken a sentient life for the first time. This is to ensure that Fildeus never curses you for it." He drew his fingers across Jesmir's left cheek. Two lines of blood marked the prince's soft face.

Jesmir recoiled in revulsion and moved to wipe his face, appalled.

"Stop!" Tamrin commanded forcefully. "Leave it till tomorrow. First blood must always be honored. It is Fildeus' commandment."

"But he doesn't deserve honor," Jesmir said. His voice quivered. "And this is blood…on my face!"

"Doesn't matter. It's no different than any other hunt. The honor isn't for him. It's for Fildeus. She requires all sacrificed life to be honored. But the first one taken is sacred most of all. You risk her curse if you don't."

Jesmir relaxed and nodded his understanding. He stared at the body that lay in a hapless heap on the ground. Rooker's blood stained the ground in darkness. A metallic odor, like copper, filled the air. Jesmir grew nauseous. He spun sideways, fell to his knees, and vomited. Tamrin watched him, a compassionate observer, and knelt down next to the prince.

"I know this doesn't help," he said. "But it was us or him. They do not intend to extend you mercy. If you hesitate, you will not survive this journey, Your Highness."

The prince nodded as he wiped the bile from his mouth.

"I have hunted before. I've just never killed another person. I didn't want to. But I had to stop his prayer. He was going to blind you," Jesmir whispered.

"How do you know that?" Tamrin asked.

"It's the same prayer he used on the captain of our ship when Brogen and his soldiers took us. And on my father before they killed him. I'll never forget it."

Tamrin looked back at the body.

"Well, it seems, Your Highness, that I am in your debt." He clapped the prince on the shoulder and stood up.

"Let's get a move on. We don't have much time if we want to meet the others in Rogue's Pointe by tomorrow night. But first, we must offer a prayer to Fildeus."

Tamrin closed his eyes, his hand on Jesmir's shoulder, and recited the *Prayer of the Blood Rite* while Jesmir stared at the dead body he'd created. When the prayer finished, Tamrin patted the prince's shoulder and stepped deeper into the woods.

Jesmir stood transfixed by the scene. He looked once more at the man on the ground. Bile rose in his throat again. He swallowed it back and ran to catch up to Tamrin, whose large steps had taken his protector thirty yards deeper into the woods.

REQUIEM FOR RESPITE

Tamrin knew it wouldn't be long before Rooker's corpse was discovered. He just didn't expect it to happen so soon. They'd barely made it a half mile when cries of dismay rang out in the distance behind them. Regardless of the short duration between their fight and now, Tamrin remained confident in the slow response time of Valshannon's guards. Valshannon relied on the power of their stone defenses over roaming patrols, and that oversight by the city authorities bought the pair much-needed time to increase the distance between themselves and the dead mercenary. Still, Tamrin spurred the prince into a sprint, himself tight on the prince's heels.

Their sprint slowed into a jog within moments, the terrain unsafe for sprints. They maintained a grueling pace, however, for a full hour before Tamrin felt confident enough to slow down. The prince never spoke during the run. Only his heavy pants of effort offered any sign Jesmir was cognizant of their situation. They were several miles into the RhineWoods by the time Tamrin called to slow their pace further. Tamrin's breath came in heavy gasps. His chest heaved. The prince had one advantage over Tamrin. He didn't have to haul a three-hundred-pound frame through the woods.

The duo slowed to a brisk walk, the silence between them awkward. Tamrin was too exhausted from the run to engage the royal in conversation. He also wasn't eager to feel ignored. Earlier attempts had met with silence and blank stares.

They pushed on through the trees for another hour. Jesmir stumbled his way over exposed roots and slick soil, following the path Tamrin showed through gestures and gasping grunts.

Jesmir didn't care what direction they traveled as long as it was away from the man he'd killed and toward his sister. He couldn't dig himself out of the spiral of despair the day brought on. Simultaneously adrift and imprisoned in his own thoughts, Jesmir felt absent from his own body. He imagined his spirit lost at sea somewhere or trapped deep inside himself, incapable of escape. He found himself incapable of more significant thought than placing one foot in front of the other.

Tamrin, unable to stand the silence any longer, chattered with mindless stories. Jesmir scrunched his face at the tracker who chose to fill the void with tales of adventures he'd been on with Shen. Tamrin was certain the prince was incognizant of his words. Still, as was his nature, Tamrin regaled Jesmir with accounts of impossible acts of heroism and bravery. Never one to give up, the big man continued his discourse without interruption. Jesmir had never heard a human being talk as much as Tamrin. The man was spewed word after word in an endless stampede of details.

After a while, Tamrin could tell his tactic had an effect because Jesmir raised his eyebrows at specific details with increased frequency.

Jesmir found himself unburdened by the grueling trek through the woods, his thoughts distracted by the words that flew from Tamrin's mouth. He slowly became grateful for the distraction and directed his focus on Tamrin's tall tales. Many of the details within Tamrin's retellings Jesmir was certain were made up—or at least well embellished. Still, Jesmir slipped for slight awareness into engaged attentiveness and was soon enthralled by Tamrin's tall tales. He couldn't pinpoint when it happened, but at some point, Jesmir noticed his anxiety over his separation from his sister receded within the comfortable vibrancy of the big man's deep voice. By midday, Jesmir listened to Tamrin in earnest, fascinated by the man's ability to wax marvelous tales so improbable he wondered if Tamrin was aware his audience found them unbelievable.

Tamrin painted mental images of impressive feats of strength and speed long into the afternoon as Ezra traveled her path along the sky and streamed beams of light through the forest canopy. The Sun Goddess's energy raised the temperature in the woods by the minute, and the humidity climbed. The air grew stagnant and musty, and their breathing grew labored. The two men continued at their brisk pace, not stopping to rest until well into mid-afternoon.

Tamrin called a halt at an outcrop of rocky terrain that edged a deep ravine. Both men, covered in sweat, collapsed onto a large rock, side-by-side. Jesmir's haggard appearance concerned Tamrin. The events of the last couple of weeks of the young man's life took a toll on the prince, and today's events had been no less harrowing.

Jesmir, no longer distracted by stories or the trudgery of placing one foot in front of the other, slipped back into thoughts of his sister and his father again. He tormented himself with actions he should have taken to save his father. The image of his father, pushed to his knees, blinded by Rooker's magic as Brogen's knife slid across the Duke's throat, replayed in his mind.

Tamrin noticed the prince's mood change and attempted to coax his charge out of the fog that re-assumed its hold with little success. Tamrin assumed the prince was beginning to recoil from the act of killing Brogen. It wasn't Tamrin's first experience with someone who fell into shock after combat. He'd even seen folks ebb and flow within the raging seas of the condition, but he'd never witnessed it so acutely as it appeared in Jesmir.

"Your Highness, drink some water," he instructed the man, who stared into the woods without acknowledgment. When Jesmir didn't respond, Tamrin tapped the young man on the knee. Jesmir jumped, startled by the contact. He blinked his eyes in rapid succession.

"Drink some water," Tamrin repeated. "There's a spring up ahead about two miles. Now is a good time to fully hydrate."

Jesmir lifted his canteen to his lips, his motion stiff. What began as slow sips turned into rapid gulps as thirst took hold. Tamrin watched as Jesmir drained the entire canteen, thankful that at least the prince tended to basic needs. The tracker took his own canteen and drank half of its contents. He extracted a strip of jerky from his pouch, tore it in half, and handed a piece to his companion.

Jesmir accepted the jerky without a word but held it loose between his knees, disinterested.

Tamrin observed Jesmir and found himself distracted by the man's appearance. Young and attractive, even alluring, if not for his near catatonia, Tamrin pictured him in the palace of Teshket amidst all manner of servants, caught in the trappings of privilege and wealth. In his current state, the black hair dye they'd used to disguise his silver locks exaggerated his pallor. Still, Tamrin thought the Prince quite handsome. His blue eyes, light skin, and natural hair color identified him as a true northerner from Teshket, where hot, bright, sunny days were rare. The prince's thin, angular jaw and wide-set eyes made it difficult to hide his royal descent. His roguish good looks also told Tamrin the prince likely suffered from no shortage of lovers.

Tamrin actually found Jesmir attractive to the point of distraction, unable to tame his own thoughts. His imagination took a turn toward the salacious. An inadvertent glance by Jesmir caused them to lock eyes, and the bigger man blushed and quickly diverted his gaze. Though the prince appeared unaware, Tamrin grew self-conscious of his thoughts and forced himself to focus on his own jerky. Tamrin chewed a chunk loose and forced his lustful thoughts away as he stared out into the RhineWoods. He lifted his chin and indicated the direction ahead.

"We'll hit the spring in less than half an hour. From there, we can head north a bit, follow the creek another mile or so, and pick up the trail that'll take us around the southern edge of Garrow's Basin."

The prince didn't respond. He stared in the direction that Tamrin indicated before he returned to looking at his hands. The pair sat in silence a while longer before

Tamrin turned to Jesmir and put his big hand on the Prince's knee. It was a gentle touch that belied the big man's intimidating appearance and size.

"I know you don't trust me yet," Tamrin started. Jesmir looked almost surprised. "But I will get you to your sister safely. I was hired to track you as part of the bounty Brogen put on you. The lie was pretty believable at the time. There was a Mayoral Seal on the warrant to legitimize Brogen's claim, so I didn't question it when I took the contract. But I trust Shen with my soul. I go where he leads. And he wants you home safe. So, I'll give my life in the effort. You have my word."

Tamrin removed his hand, rubbing both his knees with his palms. He was unsure what to do with them at the moment, and he felt awkward.

"I should have recognized the people who hired me were Killinfolk," he continued. "I would never have taken the job if I knew the man in charge was Captain Brogen. I would never willingly work for the Dark Guard."

He gave Jesmir a sideways glance, pleading. The prince, for the first time, seemed to hear Tamrin. Taken by the man's humble earnestness, Jesmir acknowledged the man who acted as his protector and relaxed.

"I'm sorry," Tamrin said softly.

Jesmir tilted his head, curious, and made an indication to speak but seemed to think better of it. Tamrin, normally talkative anyway, continued.

"I'm sorry about your father, too. That must have been horrible. No one should have to witness that."

Jesmir bowed his head and fiddled with the piece of jerky. "I was helpless to stop it," he said, finally, tears forming in his eyes. "They murdered him without hesitation. It happened so fast." He took a deep breath. "I wanted to stop them…but I froze."

Tamrin reached over and put a hand on the Prince's shoulder. "No, you didn't freeze. If it happened, as you say, there was no way you could stop it. When you are outnumbered and unarmed, and those you love are captive, there's little to do in that situation but pray. Besides, when the time came, you sprang into action and saved your sister. Without hesitation, you escaped over a cliff. That is the opposite of freezing. You saved her life and your own. As strangers in a strange land, you managed to navigate the whole of Killinshire, home of your sworn enemies, and successfully cross into Rhinestab. All while pursued by the second most dangerous killer in Conishant."

Tamrin gave Jesmir an encouraging smile.

"Second most?" Jesmir asked.

Tamrin ignored the question.

"Your Highness, I've traveled all five Realms and been in many situations where life and death hung in the balance. You didn't stand a chance at survival, and yet you somehow managed to do just that. You defied the odds. How you made it as far as you did in the RhineWoods is a blessing of the gods. Shamna's lucky twenty-three, I'd say."

Jesmir shook his head, defiant. "No, if not for Shen, our journey would have ended two days ago." He looked at his own hands. They were shaking. "Those bandits were going to…I can't even say it."

Tamrin gave a sympathetic nod. "Well, they didn't, and that's all that matters. What they tried to do to your sister didn't happen in the end. Listen, the gods help those who help themselves. You went as far as you could on your own. Shamna, in all her wisdom, gave you the luck you needed to get the rest of the way."

Tamrin snickered. "Shen may not believe in the gods, but they sure seem to believe in him. He was there because Shamna willed it. Luck doesn't happen without Shamna's blessing, Your Highness."

Jesmir shrugged. "My sister is such a devout follower of Ezra. As Teshken royals, we are supposed to bow to Shamna, but she found her strength in the Goddess of Life. Still, I think you might be right. It was the lucky twenty-three that Shen showed up when he did."

Jesmir raised his eyes to meet Tamrin's and continued.

"He's a strange one. I didn't see him fight. I was unconscious the whole time. But Jesma said he moved like a ghost. She said he was so fast that the bandits never stood a chance." He paused a moment before continuing. "I'm sure you noticed. He makes no sound when he moves. It freaks me out a bit."

Tamrin giggled. "I've known him nearly half my life. He has an uncanny knack of showing up at the right time. Sometimes, I think he doesn't believe in the gods because he is one." Tamrin's voice grew soft. "The things he does…I've never seen anyone do what he does without the faith of a believer." Tamrin paused. "Yet he does it."

Tamrin turned toward Jesmir. "That silent thing? I actually didn't know it wasn't on purpose until last night. I thought he just learned how to move like that."

"Really?" Jesmir asked, his brows furrowed.

"Yeah. He told me last night that he couldn't control it. Showed me even. It's weird."

"And he doesn't follow a god?" Jesmir asked.

"Nope. Never has. Takes his own council, creates his own luck, and for all things sacred, has more power and strength than anyone I've met in my fifty-five years in this world."

"I've never met an unbeliever," Jesmir said incredulously. "I mean, I follow Nadur, but honestly, it's never benefited me. I could see myself as an unbeliever, but it doesn't seem right. A person without a patron defies the natural order."

"He's the only one I've ever met. That I know of."

"How long have you two known each other?" Jesmir asked.

"A long time," Tamrin replied. "We met quite by accident. I was tracking a gang from Haabrestand into Rhinestab for the Haabrestand Constabulary. They'd caused enough disturbance on the trade route to draw attention to themselves. By the time I caught up to them, they'd run into their own trouble. Seems they had a reputation in Rhinestab too and drew the kind of attention nobody wants."

"The Harbinger's," Jesmir said with a nod.

"Yup. Only, I didn't know that was who he was. By the time I caught up to the gang, they'd split into two groups. I followed the group that had the misfortune of running into Shen. When I got there, all but one was dead," Tamrin continued. "Shen stood there, pissing on a tree, while the last one looked for a place to run. Shen finished, and the man turned to run right into my arms. He bounced off me like a child." Tamrin smiled as he drifted into the memory.

"You became friends after that?" Jesmir asked.

"No, not quite. Nobody becomes Shen's friend that easily. But Shen had no intention of leaving this one alive, and I didn't either. So, I dispatched that last one with a blow to the head. I told him there were more, and we teamed up to grab the rest of the gang. Took us a little over a week to get them all. I did very little of the work."

Tamrin snorted. "I should have put it together then, but I was too…" he drifts off into his own thoughts.

Jesmir watched Tamrin in silence a moment longer. Tamrin's thoughts centered on his absent friend and the love he carried for a depressed vigilante. Pain gripped his heart as he pondered how that love would never be returned in the same way. Tamrin cradled his broken heart of unrequited affection and released a heavy sigh, pushing his feelings back down. The sound caught Jesmir's attention, and the prince took his turn to observe. Tamrin peered through the canopy of leaves above at the pieces of sky peeking through and clapped his hands on his knees.

Jesmir saw it right then. In the hidden pain, Tamrin hid so well. Tamrin interrupted Jesmir's thoughts.

"Well, we best get to steppin'. There won't be much time to sleep tonight. We have a long journey ahead. I'd like to be beyond Garrow's Basin before midnight."

Tamrin shuddered at the thought of the Basin. Jesmir raised his eyebrows.

"Master Tamrin? May I ask a personal question?" Jesmir asked.

"Sure," Tamrin shrugged.

"Are you in love with Shen?"

Tamrin flinched. When he tried to speak, he stuttered, unable to form coherent words. Jesmir nodded, Tamrin's reaction confirming his suspicion.

"I suspected as much," Jesmir stated. "And you've never told anyone?"

Tamrin shook his head. "How?"

Jesmir shrugged. "I have this knack for reading people. Like an insight that I can't explain. It's why I trust you and Shen. I noticed how your eyes followed him last night and this morning." He looked Tamrin in the eye and smiled. "It's in how you talk about him too."

"I'd appreciate it if…"

Jesmir held up a hand to stop Tamrin. "I have no intention of revealing anything."

"I'd be devastated if Shen felt uncomfortable around me," he whispered. "He loves me like a brother. I'm just glad to have him in my life. As you have surmised, it's deeper than that for me. I know it will never be more than the deep friendship it is between us. But damn him, I can't help myself," Tamrin said. "He's just so damn lovable."

"Unrequited love is the worst," Jesmir whispered.

"Yeah. But I've lived with it this long. I'm fine as long as he's around."

They sat in a less uncomfortable silence for a moment.

Tamrin chuckled. "Honestly? He said something to me yesterday that makes me think he knows how I feel. It's been buggin' me ever since."

"Oh?"

Tamrin looked off into the woods, quiet again, without a response.

Jesmir changed the subject.

"Why are we avoiding Garrow's Basin if it's faster than going around?" he asked.

Tamrin frowned. "You really are a stranger in a strange land, aren't you?"

Jesmir shrugged.

"Garrow's Basin is the home of the Raysons."

"The Raysons?"

"I thought everyone in Conishant knew of the Raysons."

Jesmir just shook his head. "Never heard of them."

"They run Garrow's Basin. Some say they are half of this world and half of another. Followers of Quietius. Strange people. If they really are people. I'll be honest. I've only had one run-in with them. I felt like they were on the very edge of violence, but I could talk my way out of it. Shen has fought them enough that they leave him alone when he travels through their territory. It's uncanny, really. Quietius must like him, even though he's not a believer. The Raysons live within the mist. Shen walks through that same mist as if it's the most natural action in the world."

"I don't know much about the followers of Quietius. Never understood why living beings would want to follow the God of Death," Jesmir said.

Tamrin nodded in agreement. "I never understood why people followed Shamna over Fildeus. Give me the hunt over luck any day. Be that as it may, the Raysons are said to be half dead and half living, feeding off the life energy of the living through the help of Quietius. I don't know if it's true, but I do know I don't want to find out. My one encounter left me a bit salty."

Jesmir shuddered at the thought.

"You've encountered them before?" Jesmir asked.

Tamrin nodded. "Shen saved my ass. Showed up at the right time."

"Now I wish he was here," Jesmir said.

"Regardless," Tamrin continued, "whether truly half dead or not, I'd rather avoid them and take the extra time the long route adds. Human, half-human, or just ghosts, they are bandits first and foremost—of one form or another. They take everything from their victims. I've heard that those they don't kill, they torture and send back into the RhineWoods, naked and lost. I've heard that sometimes they send captives into the mist and hunt them for sport. The RhineWoods are dangerous enough when armed and prepared. Nearly impossible to survive naked and scared."

"Let's not go that way, then," Jesmir said, with a small amount of sarcasm in his tone.

"Agreed."

Tamrin reached up to his periapt and prayed. Fildeus responded, and Tamrin felt the furious energy within grow. His eyes glowed with a bright purple hue. He reached out along the path behind them, feeling for followers or observers. As the hot pain in his body subsided, he knew that no one followed the route they'd taken. He released the prayer, and the uncomfortable burn in his cells died out.

The two men stowed their gear in silence and headed northeast toward the promise of a spring with fresh water.

HAIR RAISING

Tamrin knew they were close to Garrow's Basin when the fog appeared through the distant trees to the north. Ezra's last bit of warm rays faded into the coldness of the evening sky. The last bit of useful light faded, and the forest slipped into the twilight hues into the color dysmorphia that hindered depth perception and made shadows move. Tamrin offered an evening prayer to Fildeus just as daylight died, and Tamrin's true sight was once again granted.

He studied the forest floor as they pushed forward. All around him, the soft glow of footprints, their colors indicative of their age, provided evidence of the recent passing of the living inhabitants of the Rhine Woods. On more than one occasion, a small splotch of color shaped like a bakru, or squirrel, passed by as the small critters scurried on in their nocturnal activities.

Tamrin enjoyed the true sight aspect of his connection with Fildeus. He pointed to a trail that he knew Jesmir could not see.

"A group of four men went through this way recently," Tamrin said.

He sensed Jesmir tense.

"How do you know?" Jesmir asked.

"True sight," Tamrin replied. "I can see their tracks. I'd say they came through about an hour ago, maybe a little longer."

Tamrin points to his right, southward off the trail.

"They went into the forest that way. Likely trappers like me. This is good trapping time. Nocturnal animals are just waking, and diurnal ones are tired and heading to their lairs."

Tamrin noted that there were other, older prints, red and purple, and many more soft, faded blues.

"This trail doesn't get much traffic. Maybe one or two folks are brave enough to come this close to the Basin every few hours or so," Tamrin said.

A bakru scuttled across the path in front of him. Tamrin almost salivated as his favorite meal escaped into the tree line of Garrow's Basin to the north. The bakru reminded him of Shen. They both shared an affinity for bakru, though Shen's affinity for the animal that shared the combined traits of squirrels, rabbits, and raccoons was not the same as Tamrin's. Shen never met a bakru he didn't like and threatened to beat the tar out of Tamrin if he ever showed up with another bakru fur.

Tamrin loved the feel of their fur and the taste of roasted bakru. But not long after the two had become friends, Tamrin trapped, skinned, and roasted one while waiting for Shen to arrive at their campsite. When Shen asked what he had on the fire, Tamrin's response was met with dismay and horror.

"How could you!" was Shen's response.

It was at that moment that Tamrin saw a part of Shen that few people ever had the chance to see. Shen was so distraught over the demise of the bakru that Tamrin almost cried with the man he thought was just a killer.

That was the last bakru Tamrin ever trapped. The lone fur he wore on his left shoulder was the very one he'd almost served Shen. Tamrin offered to burn the fur, but Shen felt it was better as an abject reminder of the promise Tamrin made to leave Shen's favorite animals alone.

"You'd look pretty nice draped around my shoulders," Shen had said. *"You hairy bastard."*

Tamrin knew Shen would never actually skin him, but he also knew it wasn't worth the risk. The thought sent a shiver down Tamrin's spine that he couldn't contain.

"You okay?" Jesmir whispered.

"Yeah, I just had a thought that I'd rather not say out loud," Tamrin whispered back as he watched the bakru disappear into the fog.

With a hand on the periapt tied into his long black beard, Tamrin spoke a silent thank you to Fildeus, Goddess of the Hunt. Tamrin never took her favor for granted. He always made his offerings to her in earnest—his requests for her blessings never came as a demand. Tamrin believed it was for this reason that he was rarely left without a response. In the rare instances Fildeus didn't pass on her blessing, Tamrin refused to fall into despair like so many others of faith tended to do. He never assumed he'd somehow fallen out of favor or that he'd been forsaken. Tamrin chose instead to believe that someone else, somewhere else, needed Fildeus' attention more, and whatever he needed at that moment was deemed easily solvable on his own.

And it usually was.

For all other problems, there was Shen.

Jesmir walked behind Tamrin with tentative steps, Tamrin's back so close he could reach out and touch the big man's furs. The light finally faded, and the whole of the RhineWoods fell into shadow. Jesmir's eyes remained locked on Tamrin's dark form, afraid to allow his gaze to transition over to the wall of mist that loomed on his left. He remained silent, scared to even speak for fear it would draw attention.

In contrast, Tamrin kept his eyes on the shadows that stalked them within the Raysons' foggy screen. He watched the mist roll closer as the trail curved southward.

The dark shadows of the Rayson clansmen paced them as the two made their way deeper into the RhineWoods. Tamrin felt the tingling in his skin spread until his entire left side grew irritated. He wanted to cancel the spell, but to do so would leave them vulnerable. For the safety of his companion, he grit his teeth and bore the discomfort. Instead, he thanked Fildeus that his beloved patron protected him.

"The Raysons are restless," Tamrin whispered.

"How do you know?" Jesmir asked.

"The fog's edge roils against whatever holds it at bay," Tamrin replied.

The tracker found it odd how the Raysons gave off no bright light in his vision. True sight revealed them when he was in the mist, but from outside, they were just dark forms like they were to everyone else. Whatever barrier kept them in the fog kept them hidden from his tracker magics. Tamrin's experience offered a more uncomfortable truth. Only the dead emitted no heat. This fact led to Tamrin's belief that the Raysons were at least partially dead.

"Stay close," Tamrin said, pointing to the fog. "They're waiting for us to stray from our path."

"Do they control the fog?" Jesmir asked with a tremble.

"I'm not sure. I just know that they attack from it. Whether they control it or use it, I've never understood."

Jesmir eyed the fog with growing fear and tightened his grip on Tamrin's heavy fur. Tamrin chuckled softly at Jesmir's childlike fear–a defensive response to the growing fear that grew inside his own mind.

"Your Highness," Tamrin whispered, "you scared?"

"A little," the prince replied.

"Well, don't worry too much. I've never seen them come out of the fog. They keep to the border."

"Why is that?" Jesmir asked, his tone skeptical.

"Again, not sure. But I've never been attacked on this trail. They've come close," he pointed at a tree four feet away. "I've seen them come about that close, but no farther." closer.

"Something stops them?" Jesmir asked.

"Don't rightly know. Just know they never have. At least not that I've seen. I don't fear the trail. But I will admit, the presence of the Raysons is unnerving."

"That's not very reassuring," Jesmir quipped, more to himself than Tamrin.

Tamrin giggled again, this time at the lighter tone in the prince's voice.

"See there," he said, "you're already doing better. Just stay close. We will be beyond the southern border of the basin in about seven miles. Then we can turn northeast."

"That far?" Jesmir cried in a hoarse whisper. "That's hours at this pace."

"Seven miles is not far at all," Tamrin replied.

Jesmir would have begged to differ, but he didn't feel like arguing the point. He knew Tamrin just wanted to calm his nerves.

Tamrin led them along the curved trail through the trees, vigilant on both sides of the trail. The darkness loomed in all directions. Jesmir could sense the trail's gradual curve to the north. He held his breath as the turn drew them closer to the foggy boundary that was now less than ten feet away. Their boots crunched on old twigs and leaves that snapped and crackled underneath their steps. Moonlight reflected through the treetops in the thinner parts of the canopy and Jesmir could make out the mist better in those moments. His neck prickled as the tiny hairs there stood on end. The fog advanced on them. This time, its line pressed closer to the trail, as far up as Tamrin indicated earlier.

"Well, hello there," Tamrin said warily. "They sure do want us to know they are here tonight. Come walk on my right, Your Highness. I don't want you to stumble in the wrong direction."

"Yeah. Yeah," Jesmir said, his voice shaky. "That's a good idea."

The mist swirled in the intermittent reflection of the larger moon. Tamrin felt the inner burn of his magic still active. His body began to feel like it was on fire, and he knew that many more eyes watched him than any previous time he'd been through here. The sensation overwhelmed his senses. He glanced at the fog to make sure it stayed put, his nerves on edge. He fought off another shiver.

Tamrin stopped in the trail and pulled Jesmir up short. The prince stumbled and almost bumped into the gigantic mass of a fur-covered tracker. Frozen in place, a deer caught in the sights of a hunter, Jesmir peered into the mist from behind Tamrin.

"What is it?"

Tamrin held up a hand to silence the prince, who complied immediately.

"I can see them moving in the fog. Something's going on in there. They are much closer to the edge of the fog than usual. I don't like how this feels. They're antsy. Waiting for something."

Dark shadows, human in form, drew closer to the edge of the mist. Tamrin couldn't be sure, but he thought he saw the tips of curved blades, the customary weapon of the Raysons, slip out beyond the barrier of the fog. Shadows of Raysons crossed in front of each other in anticipation, poised to break free. A few of the human shapes came so close to the fog's boundary that Tamrin could make out their faces, hideously grotesque, centuries of inbreeding and malice evident in the protruding jaw lines and drooping eyes. Their skin, tainted black and blue, looked as if they were bruised over the entirety of their bodies.

"I've only encountered them during the day," Tamrin says, his voice wavering.

Jesmir gulped. "That would have been nice to know hours ago. Does that mean they are different at night?"

Tamrin eyed the shadows with a shrug. He could make out curved weapons, crescent-shaped and hooked inward, unlike the normal curved blades. The Raysons swung their weapons in practiced slow arcs. He was certain that the Raysons' undivided attention was aimed in their direction. Tamrin's hair stood on end. They definitely waited for something. The thought made Tamrin more nervous than he'd ever been in the region.

Jesmir cringed, certain the forest itself was alive, with perhaps…the dead?

FIRE AND ICE

So intent was Tamrin's focus on the Raysons that he hadn't noticed that his entire body tingled all over. Jesmir was startled by Tamrin's sudden turn to inspect the rest of the surrounding forest, where the fog didn't block his perception. He searched to the east, west, and south as he cursed himself for his narrow-mindedness and for not recognizing that they likely had walked into a trap. The sensation on his skin meant that they were already surrounded. Someone lay in wait on the southern side of the trail in the distance but hid well enough so that Tamrin couldn't pick them up with his true sight. He'd been distracted, and the Raysons knew it.

With a hand on his periapt, Tamrin stretched his spell outward into the deeper shadows for signs of the trap. His cells burned with intense discomfort.

"Come on," he whispered, waving his hand forward. "Let's pick up the pace. The Raysons wait for something, and I'd rather be far away before it arrives."

"You'll get no argument from me," Jesmir replied instantly.

Tamrin walked again, brisker than before. He touched his periapt again and sent another prayer for protection to his goddess.

He noticed the first glow of a human form on the right just as the attack came.

Bright flames exploded in a wave of orange, yellow, and white. A wall of fire, taller than Tamrin, rose in front of the pair and blocked their path forward. Overcome with temporary blindness, they squinted as flames engulfed the trail ahead. Dead foliage and timbers caught fire on either side of the path. Their way was blocked.

With a reflexive shrug, Tamrin's hammer fell from the harness that held his war hammer across his back. It landed, head down, with a thud, the pommel within easy grasp at his side. But Tamrin made no move to grab the weapon. This was a magical fire. It required a magical reaction. He gripped his periapt, and his voice boomed through the forest.

"Tarake Ang Preta!" Tamrin prayed.

"Shit!" someone called from the right side of the trail.

The color of Tamrin's eyes shifted from purple to orange, and his body began to tremble violently as the new spell took effect.

Another wall of fire sprouted across the path behind them in response, the sound like the roar of crashing waves onto a rocky shore. Jesmir cried out in dismay. He looked for a way to escape and realized they were surrounded by fire on two sides and the Raysons' ominous fog on a third.

Beside him, Tamrin's body convulsed with the force of the spell the big man cast. Jesmir, helpless in the midst of the chaos, drew his sword and stood in a shaky on-guard position, his gaze toward the open forest to the south, back to the Rayson fog. The heat from the fires, the oppressive fear from the continuous presence of the mist, and the sounds that came from Tamrin as his muscles bulged and grew larger. The loud cracks caused Jesmir's hand to shake with fright.

Tamrin's body popped and snapped from inside, and his already massive frame grew larger. Tamrin cried out in a painful rage as the burning energy inside seized his mind and filled him with bloodlust. His vision blurred for a brief moment before it returned with a new focus. The colors and contrasts around him grew so acute that the individual hairs on Jesmir's head were noticeable.

Jesmir stepped back in stunned silence as Tamrin towered over him, four feet taller than he was before.

Tamrin's incisors elongated into fangs the size of iron nails and dripped saliva. His fingernails grew into hooked weapons the size of curved daggers. His hair thickened into fur like the trophies he wore in his human form.

Tamrin faced southward to where the flames originated and waited. Four men stepped from the trees. The heat from the flames, far enough away not to roast them alive, filled the space with hot air.

"Well, look what we have here," a voice resonated from the darkness on the southern side of the road. "A favored of Fildeus. I've not encountered many of you. You two seem lost."

"We ain't lost," Tamrin's replied, his tone oddly calm, almost kind. "And you'd be wise not to test us."

Taunting laughter echoed from the southern side of the road, opposite the fog wall. A small man, his skin wrinkled and old, stepped forward, his silhouette black against the flame wall ahead. He sauntered onto the trail, unafraid of the giant beast before him. His posture belied his age. The man took position at the center of the narrow trail, and firelight flickered around him, highlighting one side of his face and the other cast in shadow. His eyes, alert and youthful—much younger than the skin on his body or the gray in his hair would show—glowed red and stared at Tamrin, his countenance unfriendly. The other three men spread out onto the road, ready to flank.

The old man smiled. A chill traveled Jesmir's spine.

"Now, I'll only say this once," he said. "Please don't make me repeat myself. There's nothing worse than thickheaded warriors such as yourself making me say things twice. Put all your valuables on the ground, step back off the trail, and nobody gets hurt."

Jesmir's jaw bulged, his teeth locked in a nervous clench. With an entitled arrogance born of royal privilege, the prince raised his chin, defiant. Tamrin noted the prince's bravery. The man may not be good in a fight, but he wasn't a coward. The prince had heart. Tamrin could work with heart.

Light from the flames flickered against the slick black of Jesmir's hair dye and bathed his pale face in an inhuman glow. The tip of his sword still shook with his nerves. Tamrin, impressed with Jesmir's show of confidence, pressed his sword arm down, and the prince lowered his weapon.

"Seems you fellas, maybe picked the wrong guys to rob," Tamrin said with a smile. "We'd be happy to forget the whole thing if you'd clear a path for us. I'd personally be ever so grateful. We are in a bit of a hurry to meet with our friends in Rogue's Pointe."

"Well, look at that," the old man said. "We got a friendly mark. Don't get many of them this way. Rogue's Pointe, you say? And what business would you have there?"

Tamrin glanced around at the four men with a smile.

"Well, the usual. We intend to have some fun and maybe see if we can finagle some coin out of the visiting merchants. Possibly sign up to fight in the ring. Maybe grab a night of debaucherous pleasure. You know, the usual stuff folks do up there. You're welcome to join us if you'd like," Tamrin offered.

"Wow," said the fighter on the furthest right of his group. "This guy really is friendly."

"Yes," the older man says, "it seems our wayward friend here does have a bit of a friendly streak in him. Unfortunately for you, Beastmaster, I don't care for friendly. No offense, my friend."

Tamrin shrugged and rested his hand atop his hammer's pommel, the enormous head still on the ground. The old man raised an eyebrow and nodded his eyes.

"So, you mean to fight us all," the old man said. "And what about your companion here? Seems he's too frightened of bakru to be a warrior. Maybe we skin him and eat him."

The other three bandits laughed. Their voices echoed through the trees over the roar of the flames. More trees caught from the flames, and some smaller twigs began to pop and crackle.

"Listen, fellas," Tamrin warned, his voice rumbling deep in his chest, "as you can see, the Raysons are restless tonight, and I don't relish the thought of being caught in a brush fire. I'm sure none of you wants to end up needlessly thrown into that fog. I know I sure don't. What do you say we let each other go our separate ways today?"

The old man's maniacal laugh caused Tamrin to tense up. Something wasn't right about this guy.

"You seem to think I'm afraid of the Raysons," he stated with a laugh. "That's a mistake on your part. See, I rather like the Raysons. One of the few followers of Quietius left in Conishant. Strange lot. But you see, they make my life easy. They don't mind taking my scraps. I take your stuff. They take you. No witnesses. It's symbiotic."

Tamrin narrowed his eyes. "This is a bigger fight than you can handle. And you leave me little choice but to push through you."

Tamrin readied himself at the sound of swords being drawn. Jesmir raised his sword again. The tip wavered in the air, light from the flames reflecting off the steel that had only tasted blood once. Tamrin raised an eyebrow and nodded to the prince.

"Whatever god you pray to," he whispered, "Now is the time."

"No one ever answers," Jesmir whispered back.

Tamrin hung his head low, resigned to the fight.

"Fine," Tamrin said.

"You see, you have no hope, don't you?" the old man said, confident in his superiority. "Drop your weapons and your gear and take a step back off the road."

Tamrin's smile, when he looked up at the man, caught the villain and his companion off guard. His growl built into a roar that reverberated into the woods and shook the trees. The two walls of fire reflected off the spittle that flew from Tamrin's mouth. He crouched his eleven-foot frame and readied to attack.

"Come and grab a chunk of my ass if you can, fellas," Tamrin challenged, his voice two octaves lower than his naturally deep baritone. The vibration of his voice caused loose rocks on the ground to rumble nearby as he roared a second time.

Unintelligible chatter came from the fog, the Raysons ready in anticipation of bloodshed. It was the first time Jesmir had heard the Raysons, and he didn't like the way they sounded, like mumbled prayers. He sensed their hunger pressing out from the fog, fueling the restlessness within, and he knew the Raysons grew more agitated behind the mist.

The three men advanced a step. Jesmir stepped back, slipped, and stumbled off the trail toward the mist. Tamrin spun and snatched the prince back onto the trail and tossed him gruffly to the other side, away from the dangers of the fog. Jesmir landed on his feet and fumbled his sword. The henchman closest to the old man thrust his sword at Jesmir, who placed a lucky block as he fought to gain his footing from Tamrin's shove. His heart raced when he knocked the strike away. Jesmir released a defiant scream and readied himself. He blocked another strike. Metal on metal clanged like high-pitched bells as the two traded tentative parries.

Jesmir fought out of desperation.

His opponent fought out of confidence.

The old man held up his hands and aimed his palms at Tamrin. Tattoos of a strange symbol Tamrin had never seen before covered the inside of the man's hands. Tamrin didn't have time to study the markings as the mage began a strange chant. Neither Tamrin nor Jesmir recognized the words or style. However, they both recognized the cadence as something terrible. The old wizard's tattooed palms began to glow with fire.

"Ugh, oh," Tamrin growled.

Boots scraped across the gravel, twigs, and leaves behind Tamrin. The noise drew his attention away from the mage's spell. Tamrin yanked his hammer from the ground and swung it in a wide arc toward the rushing warriors. In his massive hands, the hammer looked like a blacksmith's tool. He swung as lightly as he could. His intent was to avoid lethality.

The two men behind him were caught off guard by Tamrin's speed and agility. Teeth bared, fangs glistening in the firelight, Tamrin faced the two men who slowed their advance in hesitation, suddenly uncertain. Their delay gave Tamrin the advantage, which he pressed, his ears focused on the wizard's words behind him, his eyes on the two in front of him. The hammer caught the leftmost man in the ribs with a sickening crunch, bones breaking inside. The man cried out in pain as he flew through the air, caught on the massive head of Tamrin's hammer.

The hammer's momentum continued, and try as he might, Tamrin couldn't slow it down. Fueled by the bloodlust within his supernatural rage, the force of the hammer swept the first man into the second. Both men cried out as they were thrown from their feet and into the menacing fog.

Howls of glee and cries of anguish echoed from the roiling mist as dark shadows, more evident in the light of the fires, descended on the two men. Metal on metal resounded as weapons clashed beyond the gray mist's edge. The men rose and stood back-to-back inside the fog, one injured beyond any ability to fight. They attempted to defend themselves from the eager Raysons, but it was over before it started.

Tamrin's arc came to rest, positioned to face the old mage with young eyes. He held his hammer in a light grip. The orange glow of his eyes caused the old man to flinch, but the mage completed his prayer, and flames flowed from his palms toward Tamrin. Tamrin dove and rolled into the woods, dangerously close to the Rayson fog. He recovered from the dive, flames scorching a portion of his fur. The acrid stench of burned hair filled the air. The big form of the beast ran before the fog, away from the mage's fire.

"Smells like someone forgot they weren't supposed to play with fire," the mage taunted.

Tamrin kept quiet as the mage stepped forward. The heat of the flames singed Tamrin's lungs, and he gasped at the painful inhalation of hot air. Flames licked the forest all around and threatened to burn out of control. Small patches of dead leaves and branches ignited, and the trees themselves caught fire.

Tamrin prepared to lunge forward toward the mage when another cone of flames swept a wide arc across the trees in front of him, engulfing more of the surrounding foliage. Tamrin ran ahead of the arc, barely able to maintain a safe distance along the fog line. The mage's sweeping flames chased Tamrin along the edge of the fog until the big man was safely out of range.

Tamrin's muscles tensed, and he prepared to exit the tree line near the second wall of fire. With a powerful crouch, Tamrin lunged forward but froze in place, unable to move.

Cold—colder than any coldness he'd ever felt gripped the big man's arm. He looked down and saw an icy hand holding his, its source within the fog. Terror seized the big man as thoughts broke into his mind unbidden. He knew not where they came from, but they frightened him with their proximity.

Relax, warrior, we mean you no harm. Come join us. We could use a man with your talents. Join us and bring us the mage. You will be rewarded.

Tamrin looked down at the fingers that gripped him. Hard, blackened nails pressed into his flesh. Rough, torn fingers, openly seeping some clear liquid like the plasma in blood, held him fast. The gold radiated up his arm and down toward his hand. Tamrin tried to shake loose from the icy grip. The chill drained Tamrin of his own will. He struggled to push against the voice.

Do as we ask, and no harm will come to you. Refuse us, and you will pay.

Tamrin's knuckles and elbow began to ache. His grip on the hammer weakened, and the pommel slipped from his grasp. The cold worked its way toward his shoulder. In a panic, he let out a frightened growl and twisted his massive frame away from the hand with all of his strength. His rear leg pushed forward, and his hips twisted. The hand refused to release, and the force of Tamrin's motion, enhanced by his bloodlust and beastly form, yanked the dark body of the Rayson from the fog. The Rayson lost its grip. Its nail ripped Tamrin's flesh as the Rayson flew toward the mage.

Tamrin didn't hesitate. He gripped his hammer, his hand stiff and arthritic. He rushed in a direct path that would take him right past the Rayson that tumbled through the air, its face contorted in rage at the affront. As the gap closed between them, the Rayson landed and turned back to the enraged Tamrin, ready to fight.

Tamrin paused.

That's no Rayson. What the hell is that thing? He thought to himself.

Before Tamrin could reason out the horror that threatened him, the creature leapt, its curved blade held in a two-handed overhead grip. Tamrin dropped his hammer, brought his clawed fingers up, and jammed them forward. The creature's eyes opened wide, its mouth contorted in shock at the ease with which the beastly man seized the advantage. Tamrin's spiked claws caught the creature in the ribcage, impaling it. The creature writhed in Tamrin's massive grip, still bringing the sword down.

Blood oozed onto Tamrin's hand. His fingers felt the effects of frostbite. With a frightened roar, Tamrin swung his arm and sent the wounded monster toward the wall of fire at the rear of the trap.

The creature had more mass than Tamrin anticipated. That or the cold affected his strength. The creature landed short of the flames and effortlessly slid backward, both feet on the dirty trail, its blade digging into the ground. It came to rest just in front of the wall of flame.

Tamrin retrieved his hammer and stepped toward the Rayson. The old man, his first two spells exhausted, chanted another. The black form, its pale-yellow eyes darting from Tamrin to the mage, screamed with a sound so high-pitched and painful to the ears that Jesmir, the mage, and the one remaining henchman cried out. They clasped their hands to their ears. The scream, filled with malice and fury, caused the entire forest to go silent for miles. Tamrin stood, unaffected by the sound, immune to the fear induced by the scream.

"Thank you," Tamrin snarled.

The mage's prayer caught in his throat as the Rayson's anguished shriek stunned its victims, their muscles seized in fright. The incantation died in the air. Jesmir, restrained by the mage's henchman, was unable to shake off his captor during the fear-inducing wail. Frozen, his eyes wide with horror, he stared at the threat that engaged with Tamrin. The henchman recovered before Jesmir could free himself and tightened his grip on the defenseless prince.

The monster's wail faded, and it readied its curved sword, black metal glinting in the firelight. Its muscles rippled and crouched again, ready to attack. Blood oozed from the five large holes in its ribcage, red as any human's—but the Rayson stood its ground, unphased by its injuries. Its black and blue skin reflected in the fire, and beads of sweat formed on its naked body.

Whatever this was, Tamrin noted, it lived. It bled. He took solace in the knowledge that anything that bled lived and that which lived could be killed.

Tamrin advanced, his right arm still struggling from the paralysis induced by the icy grip; the fingers in his left hand stiffened, the joints tight from the cold that seeped into them from the blood of his enemy. Tamrin ignored the pain and gripped his hammer, the large wooden head pointed toward the ground.

The wizard recovered from the magic-induced fear and smirked as Tamrin reengaged in combat with the Rayson. The monster lunged forward, his blade poised to strike. Its pale-yellow eyes were intent on Tamrin, who waited for his opponent to make the first move. Dark and muscular, the Rayson rushed. Tamrin feigned with his hammer, and the creature dodged. But Tamrin's attack never came. The big man switched tactics and stepped forward, his hips twisting with power, and kicked the Rayson with the full weight of his massive body. The creature flew through the night, its scream high-pitched and filled with rage. The Rayson fell into the slowly fading flames that still blocked the road.

The wizard watched in shock as the creature evaporated into a mist upon impact with the flames. Its final wail died into the night. Tamrin turned to the wizard and smiled, his fangs dripping with saliva.

"You still want to dance?" he snarled, his voice filled with gravel, deeper than before, reverberating off the trees.

The old mage held up his hands, tattoos aimed at Jesmir, eyes locked with Tamrin.

"You seem to care about this one," he said coldly. "One step closer, and he dies."

The wizard's henchman cried out in dismay. "Wait! I'm here too!"

"You are of little consequence," the mage replied.

"Say one more word, mage," Tamrin warned, "And my hammer will sever your head from your shoulders."

"You can't keep the bloodlust up forever, hunter," the mage replied.

"Longer than you can, your flames," Tamrin mocked. His grin grew wider. Tamrin could feel the hunger threatening to take permanent hold but resisted the temptation. "I'm favored by Fildeus. Want to see how much so?"

The man considered Tamrin's words as the two stared at each other, gaging the threat each presented. The old man laughed. It was hearty and deep. Then he looked toward his henchman.

"Let the sniveling little man go," the old man told the younger fighter.

The henchman looked back and forth between Tamrin and his employer. He appeared to consider some other option but ultimately chose to comply with the command. Jesmir turned and punched the henchman in the jaw. The strike caught the henchman off guard, and his head snapped back. The henchman held his jaw for a moment and glowered at the prince. As he recovered, he put his sword to the Prince's neck.

"I should just kill you where you stand," he whispered.

Jesmir, his body shaking, stared the man in the eyes and whispered back to him.

"Do it."

The henchman tilted his head and looked at the mage, who watched. Tamrin growled a low rumble that reverberated in his chest and echoed off the canopy of trees.

"Enough, Erol," the mage said. "Let these two go. Today is not our day." He turned to Tamrin. "We will let you pass if you let us go our own way. Do you accept this truce, or shall we continue?"

Tamrin looked at Jesmir, who stepped closer to his protector and retrieved his sword from the ground. He pointed the tip at the henchman with more confidence. Tamrin flexed his big, magic-enhanced muscles in acknowledgment. The wizard nodded at the henchman and stepped back the way he came, eyes locked with Tamrin, his smile twisted and menacing.

"You fought well, hunter. Not many survive an encounter with me. You truly are favored by Fildeus. I'll give you that. Be warned. I am favored in my way. Pray for both our sakes we never meet again."

The wizard disappeared into the woods south of the trail. Tamrin watched, his True Sight still active, until he could only see the glowing tracks of the wizard and his last remaining henchman disappear in the distance. Tamrin looked down at Jesmir to confirm the prince wasn't hurt. The wizard's voice echoed through the trees, coming from the darkness.

"Although, I hope we do. It would be a glorious battle, favored of Fildeus! But I doubt we shall see each other. You have quite the surprise ahead of you!" Laughter followed for a few moments before it finally died off.

As the voice faded into the night, Tamrin fell to his knees and released the blood lust. His body shrank back to its normal size, and the orange tint on his eyes faded to purple. The purple faded into its natural brown color, and Tamrin fell forward onto the trail with a thud.

His fangs retracted, and the long claws returned to the soft, gentle hands Jesmir had already grown used to. A slow groan escaped Tamrin's lips. Jesmir rushed to him and knelt beside the beleaguered tracker.

"Master Tamrin, are you okay?" he asked. Fear and worry colored his words.

Tamrin shook his head slowly.

"No. But I will be. That Rayson's touch was pretty bad. But the bloodlust is worse. It hurts everywhere. I just need a moment."

Jesmir looked around in panic. The walls of flame died out as he watched. The magic that held the fire alive ebbed out, and even the small fires, fueled by tinder, died. Jesmir couldn't reason out why.

Darkness returned to the woods, and both men's eyes took time to adjust. He turned and looked back at the fog that still pressed the line of trees, harder to see after in the darkness. He couldn't make out the shapes of the Raysons beyond but cringed in fear at the knowledge of their presence.

As despair gripped him, he looked down at Tamrin, who rested with his head bowed, still on his knees, hands on the ground, his breath labored and heavy. Jesmir chastised himself for his lack of prowess, his fear, and his weakness.

"This isn't the man I want to be," he said to Tamrin quietly.

Tamrin glanced at him sideways and smiled. "Don't be so hard on yourself. I've been where you are, too, Your Highness."

"Jes, my friends call me Jes," he says.

Tamrin smiled at Jesmir. "Tam. My friends call me Tam."

Jesmir smiled for the first time since Tamrin met him. It was a dazzling and friendly smile, sincere and light. Tamrin saw, in that moment, a different measure of the man he protected, and he liked what he saw.

"Let me help you up," Jesmir said, and he gripped Tamrin's arm.

"Thanks," the big man replied, grateful for the help. As he rose, he placed his hand on Jesmir's shoulder once more. "How about we practice with that sword of yours after we get to Rogue's Pointe?"

"I don't think I have that much ability there," the Prince said.

"What do you have skill with?"

"Well, I'm a damn good shot with the bow," the prince replied.

Tamrin let out a belly laugh, deep and joyful. "Why didn't you say so? You really do hunt?"

Jesmir nodded, "I do. Did you think I made that up?"

"Hmm." Tamrin fumbled through his pack and withdrew a leather necklace with a periapt on it. "You said you follow Nadur?"

"I do. But she doesn't seem to like me much."

"Well, that's because I think you are not following the right goddess. Here, put this on. While we walk, let me regale you with the great tales of Fildeus, the Wild Huntress, and my favorite bi-annual event, the Wild Hunt. She's who every hunter should pray to, Your Highness. That's why you haven't found your strength. You have the heart of a hunter. No other god suits you."

Jesmir took the periapt of Fildeus and, unable to see it in the dark, placed it over his head and tucked it inside his blouse.

"The Wild Hunt?" he asked Tamrin, his voice raised an octave in curiosity.

Tamrin's laugh boomed again, boisterous, filled with mirth. Clasping Jesmir on the back with a solid thud, he propelled the Prince forward on their path. He filled the darkness with lavishly embellished stories of the Wild Hunts he'd experienced as they walked.

Tamrin kept one eye on the fog to his left. The Raysons still lurked behind the screen, their dark silhouettes still on the prowl. They continued to follow the trail, leery of the fog.

"What the fuck are the Raysons, exactly?" Jesmir asked.

"I wish I knew," Tamrin's voice quivered.

Jesmir didn't like the fear he sensed in his protector. If Tamrin was frightened, then Jesmir knew whatever the creatures behind the fog were, it wasn't good. He made sure to keep Tamrin between him and the wall of fog just inside the woods.

ODDS NETHER IN FAVOR

"**H**old up," Tamrin said.

Jesmir sensed the rise in stress within Tamrin's voice and complied. His heart rate sped up in anticipation of some new danger he couldn't sense.

"What is it?" the prince asked.

Tamrin's eyes once again glowed a light purple. The telltale signal of his true sight was active again. Jesmir huddled close to Tamrin while the big man scanned the area ahead and to the right. The forest canopy was too thick to allow the night sky to shed any light on the trail, and Jesmir's eyes struggled to fully adjust. He could discern some details a yard or two away but not much more.

The world beyond was little more than blackness on darker shades of blackness. Forced to rely on Tamrin's true sight as a bystander, he whispered in desperation.

"What do you see?" Jesmir's voice now reflected the quiver that Tamrin's held prior.

Tamrin's head swept the forest's southern section and seemed to freeze just ahead on the trail. Jesmir couldn't see it, but he sensed by the tension in Tamrin's body that the tracker was focused on something in particular.

"Shit," Tamrin said and pointed ahead.

Jesmir's heart sank. Whatever it was, he knew he wouldn't like the answer.

"What is it?" he asked Tamrin.

The tracker, unsure how much more the prince could take, was reluctant to answer. Tamrin was certain that Jesmir would know how bad the news was as soon as he revealed it. He just wasn't sure how the man would react.

Tamrin stared into a dark black void. Its border crawled across the ground ahead like a venomous vapor, the edge of its border visible in his true sight just around a bend to the left. It rolled low to the ground, barely a foot tall, like a fog, slow and thick. It settled onto the ground at its border. The soft, warm glow of the trees around him transitioned into total blackness, where the void blackness of the vapor began. With a heavy sigh, he shook his head in resignation.

A netherstack blocked their path ahead.

"We can't go that way," he said to Jesmir.

"What do you mean?" Jesmir demanded.

"Netherstack."

"Krikhi's tits," Jesmir exclaimed, his voice carrying deep into the woods.

Tamrin turned and scanned the forest to his right for signs of the mage or any other danger. He stepped toward the southern edge of the path. Footprints of all shapes and colors slowly faded as the night air cooled the ground. There were no signs of a possible ambush. He turned to Jesmir, the smaller man's face a collection of red and orange hues. Tamrin could see the blood rush to Jesmir's cheeks and ears.

"It's going to be okay, Your Highness," Tamrin replied. "Stay close, but don't trip me up."

The prince nodded. Tamrin approached the bend in the road with slow, deliberate steps. As they drew closer and the bend straightened, Tamrin spotted the source of the mist void. Just inside the tree line, to the right of the trail opposite the Rayson fog, a collection of black fingers pointed skyward. The void mist spewed from their tips and rained down around them. Seven stacks sat inside the tree line. They were close enough that Jesmir could make out the darker space within the natural darkness of the forest.

Tamrin sighed. He'd been through this area less than two seasons ago, but this group of netherstacks was not there at that time. This was a new formation. Tamrin was more concerned with how quickly they'd multiplied. He'd never seen so many in one place that wasn't known to be decades old.

"What do we do?" Jesmir asked.

"Well, this formation goes deep into the forest," Tamrin said and pointed to the right. "None of the trees show life for several hundred yards into the forest. It's possible that what I see is just the beginning of the nether. We'll have to circumnavigate. But I don't know how far. There's no way to reach Rogue's Pointe by tomorrow if we head south. We'll lose time we can't afford to lose."

Damn that mage, Tamrin thought.

"Well, we best get moving," Tamrin said. "No sense in dilly-dallying."

Tamrin stepped forward. He was stopped by a frantic tap by Jesmir on his arm. Tamrin turned toward Jesmir, whose attention was directed toward the Rayson's side of the trail. Tamrin sensed the danger before he saw it. The prince, frozen in fear, turned to look at Tamrin as the wall of fog surged beyond the imaginary barrier that Tamrin indicated.

"Oh shit," Tamrin gasped. He released his genuine sight spell and attempted to pray the hunter's prayer.

Before the words could escape his mouth, the wall of fog engulfed the pair in a cool gray mist that froze the words in Tamrin's throat. Screams of victory surrounded them, and both men collapsed from an unseen blow to the back of their heads.

"Well, now, isn't that something? Looks like we have some fresh genetics to add to the family gene pool." It was the last words Tamrin heard before he succumbed to unconsciousness.

HUNTER GAMES

Tamrin woke to a throb at the back of his skull. He was surprised to find himself tucked away in the comfort of a soft bed made of stacked furs. He stretched his body as if he'd woken from a strange dream. His muscles ached, and he assumed he'd slept harder than he intended. He wasn't quite sure where he was. The dream was so vivid it felt like a full day of life had passed. He remembered some details, though they were fuzzy. He had the nagging suspicion that he'd drank too much the night before and missed the reveille call with the rest of the search party.

If the voices and noises that surrounded him were any sign, he really had overslept. It sounded like the rest of the team were breaking down camp.

Had it all really been a dream? He thought.

He sure hoped so. Tamrin opened his eyes and was surprised by the thick fog that had moved in while he slept. Odd how the presence of fog had made its way into his nighttime visions. His body ached as if from over-exertion. Memories of the crazy dream flooded back, and he recalled a fight with a mage and the frigid grip of the Raysons on his arm. His arm ached with the memory like some strange carryover from the dream world to the physical realm. With a groan, he stretched again.

His head hurt something awful. He touched the back of his crown and winced with shock and pain. He'd been hit over the head.

The metaphorical fog in his brain cleared, and he bolted upright, alert and ready to fight. He looked down at himself and saw that he slept on a bed of furs. Furs he didn't recognize as his own. All around him, the pale mist of fog flowed, thinning enough for brief moments that he could see people busy at work. The mist would thicken again, and the human forms would fade into fog-screened shadows. Through the mist, torchlights flickered, their light a reflected halo blurred by the fog. With careful movements, he reached out his hands to feel around his environment, desperate to locate his hammer. Dark shadows moved in the mist, and he immediately recognized them as Rayson.

It wasn't a dream.

Surprised to find he wasn't restrained, he rolled over and pushed himself to his feet. Visibility through the fog was barely ten feet. Throughout the infinite distance of the mist, even in the dark, he could see more defined forms mill about. Most engaged in a task of some sort. Yellow rings, the reflective nature of light on fog, felt brighter than they otherwise would in a typical environment.

There were more dark shadows than what they'd seen when he and Jesmir were on the trail. Another memory triggered, and Tamrin realized he was within the Raysons' camp.

And this time, there's no Shen, he thought. A twinge of fear fell over him. He reached up to touch his periapt to pray for true sight and gasped. He felt the loose hairs of his beard. Tamrin never left his beard loose. His heart sank. His periapt was gone.

He searched around for his hammer but could not find it in the immediate vicinity.

Jesmir!

"Jes!" he whispered.

The response from behind startled him.

"I couldn't risk your use of magic. That monstrous form of yours is quite a fright," a man said.

Tamrin spun, ready to fight a dark monster like the one he'd dispatched in his fight with the mage. Instead, before him stood a very normal man. He was average in almost every way. Average height, average build, averagely unremarkable. The only remarkable thing about him was how apparently poor his hygiene was. The man looked as if he'd never been graced with soap, a safe place to sleep, a healthy diet, or medical care. His smile was a jagged mix of broken and missing teeth. The few teeth he'd managed to retain pointed in odd directions, and most were black. In the case of the last remaining front lower tooth, it was both. His nose was slightly bent and pushed to one side–likely, Tamrin gathered from one too many fights. His eyes tilted downward in a somewhat exaggerated manner like they threatened to slide off his face. His hair and beard were a scraggly mess, thin and wispy. Gnarled, calloused knuckles and fingers showed a life of hardship. His nails were cracked and yellow.

Dressed in tattered pants and an open tunic, his sternum protruded in a way that left Tamrin wondering when it was the man who had last eaten any actual food.

Oddly, the man didn't smell nearly as horrible as he appeared. In fact, Tamrin noted, the man smelled like sage and woodland herbs.

Now this looks like a Rayson, he thought.

The man held out Tamrin's periapt of Fildeus up for a moment before pocketing it away.

"You need to give that back to me," Tamrin scowled.

"In due time," the man said. "Maybe."

"Where is my friend?" Tamrin asked.

"Also in due time," the man said.

Tamrin stepped toward the man and grabbed him by the throat. The man didn't react in the slightest. He raised an eyebrow, eyes locked with his prisoner. Tamrin sensed motion in the mist that swirled and thickened around him. Dark shadows grew and gained detail as they approached. From within the fog, several curved blades, similar to the one the creature on the road carried, came into focus inches from vital organs and arteries.

"You see," the man croaked against the tight grip on his neck. "There's no chance you can fight us all. If we wanted to kill you, we'd have done so already."

Tamrin squeezed tighter, and the shadowed blades drew closer. He felt a pinpoint of pressure on the small of his back, at the base of his spine.

"You like walking?" the man said. "The blade at your back can sever your spinal cord before you have a chance to kill me. You'd never walk again. In fact, you may spend your life shitting your pants, unaware you'd ever done so."

Tamrin fought the urge to kill the Rayson and released his grip.

"If anything happens to my friend," Tamrin threatened. "I'll kill the lot of you."

"Many have tried," the man said with no sarcasm.

"What do you plan to do with us?" Tamrin asked.

"Depends," the man said.

"On?"

"On what you can offer us in return for your freedom," the man said. The man waved the others away, and Tamrin felt the knife on his back release its threatening pressure.

He watched as the Raysons turned and walked back into the mist.

"Walk with me," the man said.

Tamrin obliged.

"Do you know who we are?" he asked.

"Yes," Tamrin replied. "You are the Raysons. Thieves, murderers, and unchallenged rulers of Garrow's Basin."

The man bounced his head with something less than a nod. Tamrin suspected that his perception did not quite fit what the man wanted.

"Is that not what you meant?" Tamrin asked.

"It is accurate, in its own way," the man replied. "Yes, we are the Raysons. And yes, we hold Garrow's Basin as our homeland. And yes, we steal and murder and do many of the things we are known for. But we do it to survive." The man stopped and pointed at Tamrin. "Calling us thieves and murderers, on the other hand, is rather reductive. We protect what is ours, including our own existence."

"And how do you decide what is yours?" Tamrin asks.

"How do you?" the man returned.

"I'm not interested in your games. I've met some of you once before."

"Have you now? That seems unlikely. No one has ever escaped us," the man said. "You'd be one of us if you'd encountered us."

"You sure about that?" Tamrin asked.

The Rayson regarded Tamrin for a moment.

"Well, one has. But you are not he," the man replied.

Tamrin raised an expectant eyebrow, but the Rayson did not react or reply.

"I travel in rarified circles," Tamrin offered.

"Do you now?" the man asked.

Tamrin didn't elaborate. He didn't recognize this man from his previous encounter and wasn't sure of his position within the clan. Shen always said that with the Raysons, it was best to reveal things in stages. Tamrin opted to keep the conversation discordant.

"To answer your question about how I decide what is mine is simple. I earn what I have. I do not take what belongs to others," Tamrin said.

The Rayson scoffed. "Do you not take the pelts from animals that have done nothing to you? I'd say that the bear whose hide you wear on your shoulders would feel you had taken something that wasn't yours."

"I hunt to provide food, clothing, and to make a wage," Tamrin replied.

"As do we. You hunt animals. We hunt people."

"I'm sorry?" Tamrin said.

"Ah, the crux of it," the man smiled. "You are a follower of Fildeus. You understand the hunt better than most. Have you partaken in the Wild Hunt?"

Tamrin swallowed and nodded.

"Good. Then you will understand this better. I offer you choices. Something you never offer your victims. Your skills against ours. If you win, you and your friend go free. If you lose, you die. Your friend still goes free."

"And what if I choose not to partake?" Tamrin asked.

"Then you both die. Well, you die. Your friend will drink your blood in a special ritual and become one of us. We are in need of new members. Our gene pool has become rather shallow thanks to the infertility of our male offspring. We need new males to improve the genetic variability and hopefully break the infertility cycle. And well, your companion looks to be of very fine and fertile bloodlines."

"He'll never agree to that," Tamrin replied.

"We don't need him to agree. We'll tie him down onto the altar of Quietius and force your blood into his mouth. Drown him in it if we have to," the man said. When the man said this, his eyes shimmered like the misty air that surrounded them.

"Don't worry," the man said. "You'll have your hammer to defend yourself. Just not your periapt. No magical incursion from your patron tonight. Tonight, it's Hunter vs Hunters."

"Trust me when I tell you, this is not the choice you want to make," Tamrin said.

"Why is that?" the man responded.

"I told you, I travel in certain circles few travel in. Harm us, and you'll invoke the wrath of the Harbinger."

The man searched his surroundings as if he expected the sudden appearance of a ghost he didn't believe was there. Unphased by Tamrin's invocation, he pointed to a flickering light in the mist behind him.

"Not the first time someone said that. Won't be the last. He ain't here right now, from what I can tell. What I know of the Ghost of the RhineWoods, he doesn't have friends either."

Tamrin wasn't surprised by the man's response, though he'd hoped for more consideration.

"Now," the Rayson continued, "your gear, minus your periapt, sits and waits for you at that light there." He pointed again at the light he'd indicated earlier. "I suggest you grab your items and make the run for your life. We will keep your friend until the hunt is over. Survive or not, as long as you partake in the hunt, he will be free to go upon your demise."

Tamrin glared at the man. A low growl rumbled in his chest. The man smirked, daring the big man to attack. Tamrin clenched his fists and jaw. From the way the man spoke, Tamrin knew he had no intention of allowing either of them to leave Garrow's Basin.

The man acknowledged Tamrin's anger.

"Oh, you could most certainly kill me. But then your friend's life is forfeit if you do."

Tamrin saw little advantage in his position. He knew he had no choice but to buy time through compliance. One Rayson was tough to beat. A handful, or worse, an entire clan, wasn't something he thought he could take on. Especially if they all could turn like the one he'd ripped from the fog. Through the foggy view, he'd already counted over twenty. Who knew how many more there were? He'd never be able to kill them all. And he'd never get to Jesmir before whoever held him sounded an alarm. With quiet resignation, he stepped past the man to retrieve his gear. He was one step beyond the man when he paused.

"You the leader of this clan?"

"I am," the man said.

"Then, one thing before I go," Tamrin said.

"What is that?" the man asked.

Tamrin whirled around with a hard right hook. His massive fist, almost as big as the man's head, slammed into the Rayson's temple. Tamrin followed through with his punch, his full power behind the strike. The man fell sideways into the mist and dirt. Far enough away, Tamrin could barely make out the man's features.

"We have a fighter!" the man cried from his position on the ground. "We shall enjoy this hunt, hunter."

Maniacal laughter rang out from all around the camp. Tamrin realized he was surrounded. Disgusted and dismayed, he hurried toward the light shown by the man to retrieve his gear. As he gathered his belongings, he planned his strategy.

I have to find a way to circle back and locate Jesmir.

PRINCE STOUTHEART

Jesmir sat held against a tree by several loops of rope. He'd awaken to a foggy sense of vertigo. The back of his head was tender to the touch, a fact he learned when he leaned his head against the rough bark of the tree to which he was tied. It took him a few times to learn the lesson, and he finally stopped, causing himself further discomfort, and refrained from resting his head back. The position was already uncomfortable, but now the muscles between his shoulder blades were beginning to burn from his limited range of motion.

He'd tried to call out to Tamrin occasionally, but all it did was draw the attention of the filthy-looking Raysons that held him captive. Several women, their teeth black or chipped, dressed in ragged clothes, came by and leered at him from the swirling fog that surrounded him. Even if they hadn't been dirty or had rotten teeth, he could tell they were not attractive in the slightest. Yet they ogled him with such lust he couldn't help but fear their intentions.

With frantic motions, he'd tried to scope his surroundings, but the mist was too thick to pierce. The haze of moisture that surrounded him soaked into his clothes and gathered on the rope in little beads. Dark shadows moved in the distance like shades of souls, their presence all around him among the blurred halos of torchlights.

He struggled against the rope, but the noise drew attention to him and brought the Raysons around. He had no idea how long he sat in his current state, but it felt like an eternity.

"He's a tasty morsel, I dare say," one woman said.

"That black hair is so shiny," another said, "and his eyes. Did you see how blue they are? I won't mind taking that from him. I could stare at them forever. I can smell the fertility on him."

"I hope his friend refuses so we can start the Ritual now," the first woman added. "I don't want to hunt. I want to bed this one."

"No, we need the hunt. I'm sure Brill has convinced him that we'll let his friend go if he partakes," said the second.

"We'll know soon enough," a third replied.

Jesmir didn't understand the whole meaning contained within their conversation, but he understood the intent. He understood enough to know Tamrin was still alive, but maybe not for much longer. Jesmir lamented his personal uselessness in a fight. He wished he had taken his father's admonishments more seriously. If he'd only given more to the combat training, like his father had asked, like his sister had, then he'd be more adept in this situation. He fought the frustrated urge to bang his head against the tree to which he was tied.

Why do I have to be so fucking useless? He thought.

His father, kind as he was, never understood Jesmir's constant need for a good time. Jesmir understood now.

"I'm sorry, father," he whispered under his breath. "I know I've disappointed you."

The events of the last few weeks were more than adequate to convert Jesmir's thoughts on the subject, but three weeks weren't enough to make anyone a warrior. At thirty-two years old, he'd shirked the responsibilities of his position for so long that he'd grown soft in his heart. Though his body was lean and decently in shape, he was useless in a fight, and now, the affable and valiant Tamrin would pay the price.

His sister had almost paid the price.

If not for Shen, they'd both be dead, and his sister would have suffered all the more for it.

I'm fucking useless.

A woman emerged from the mist and knelt before him. Her hair was a wild, knotted mess, light brown with twigs tangled into it. From her neck dangled a stone with a skull on it. The periapt of Quietius.

Her breath smelled of rot and infection. She looked barely in her twenties, yet Jesmir couldn't imagine there was much more life left in her. Her gaunt and malnourished face hovered inches from his. Her hollow, sunken eyes studied him with the curiosity of a curator. Dirt covered her face, making the lines stand out more.

Yet she smelled a lot like junipers. It was an odd duality. She smelled lovely, but she looked wretched except for her breath.

"I think I'm going to partake of you first after the Ritual," she said with a smile. "I hope you don't die in the process. I really want my baby to have blue eyes like yours." She rubbed her lower belly. "I'm ready."

"Baby?" Jesmir asks, aghast.

With her dirty hand, she ran a yellow fingernail along the side of his cheek.

"You are so handsome," she whispered. "So virile."

Jesmir shuddered at the thought of her implication.

A distant thud caught each of their attention, and they looked toward the source. In the distance, a commotion broke, hidden by the fog. Jesmir recognized the rumble of Tamrin's voice and heard his signature growl. Then Jesmir heard laughter, not Tamrin's gregarious laugh full of hope and joy but a more sinister, evil laugh from someone else in the same vicinity as Tamrin. The girl snapped her head to look in the direction of the other woman with a smile.

"Good, it's begun!" she called out.

The other women whooped with loud cattle calls. The dirty girl turned back to Jesmir. "Don't go far. It'll all be over soon. Then you and me can make three."

Jesmir tried to shrink back from the horror before him as the woman transformed from a dirty girl into a creature with black and blue skin. Her eyes turned a pale yellow, and her hair turned gray. From behind her back, she pulled a curved blade. A loud scream, high-pitched, sounded in the distance like a call to arms. She responded in kind.

Jesmir felt the chill of terror grip him. He wanted to cover his ears, but he dared not move. His heart raced, and adrenaline surged from the fear, the same fear that gripped him during Tamrin's battle just hours ago.

Without a word or a glance toward the tied-up prince, the woman sprinted toward the first scream. In the mist, Jesmir saw others run by, headed in the same direction. A sinking feeling came over him, and he suddenly realized what she meant by "the hunt."

Tamrin was in trouble.

And he, the useless prince, was tied to a tree.

He searched into the mist for any signs of shadows in motion. He called out into the void of swirling droplets. No one came. He sighed in relief that he was alone. All around him, the mist swirled. At first, he wasn't sure, but it appeared as if the foggy barrier thinned with each passing moment. Details around him revealed themselves as the flickering blurred torchlights cut through the fog with greater intensity. Torches, mounted on thick poles, scattered through the trees. As the mist gave way, Jesmir realized it moved with the Raysons wherever they went.

Whatever these creatures were, the mist followed them.

The light of the torches that surrounded him flickered off moisture nearby and caught his attention. His sword, bow, and quiver of arrows sat on the ground near to him. With a sigh of relief, he began to strain against his restraints in earnest.

The rope that held him dug into his skin through his clothes. He felt the abrasions form. He paused as the skin in his right biceps burned. Jesmir gritted his teeth and continued to work his body. The bark against his back ripped at his clothes. He heard the material rip behind him. Yet he continued to struggle.

He resisted again the urge to bang his head against the tree in frustration. He stopped and gathered his breath, his chest heaving with exhaustion. He let out a deep breath and noticed the rope contained more slack than it had before. I looked at the braided strands and realized the beads of moisture had soaked in. New ones formed, and he watched as the rope became more saturated from the mist in the air. With all of his strength, he strained against the ties that bound him. He continued to twist and push. A trickle of blood ran down his back.

He stopped, released all his breath, and held back a celebratory laugh. The rope had stretched further. He twisted his torso to push his right shoulder against the tree. The rugged bark dug into him more, and his back bled more. Still, he twisted harder—desperation his motivation. Desire to help his sole mission. The rope dug into his left shoulder now, and still he twisted.

The tension gave way. When he relaxed a third time, the rope had loosened enough to give him room to maneuver. Jesmir wasted no time. He wiggled himself down until the rope was at his chin. His head smacked the tree, and he winced from the impact against the lump, but he pushed through.

It took several minutes–minutes he was sure Tamrin didn't have, but finally, Prince Jesmir broke himself free of his restraints. He wasted no time. He hurried to his gear. There, on top of his quiver, laid the periapt of Fildeus that Tamrin had given him. He gripped it and prayed with all his might. He begged Fildeus to grant him magic.

But no answer came.

"I don't know why I thought you'd be any different," he mumbled.

Jesmir stuffed the stone emblem into his pocket and threw on his sword and quiver. He looked in the direction the woman and other shadows ran.

"You may not be good in a fight, Jesmir," he whispered. "But Shamna be damned if I'll abandon the person who looks out for me."

Jesmir readied an arrow and ran after the monsters that hunted the hunter.

HUNTED HUNTER HUNTS

Tamrin hurried through the mist, unsure of just how far he'd get before the creatures followed. He was certain of only two things—he made an enormous shadow in the fog that was hard to hide, and he had no intention of leaving Jesmir behind. All in all, neither detail constituted a valuable plan of escape. But he always liked to start with what he knew, which, he admitted to himself, wasn't much.

His previous encounter with the Raysons, several years ago, was very different. The leader was a different man than the one he'd just met. At that time, it was a simple matter of invoking the presence of Shen. Easily done when Shen stood next to him.

How did I not pick up on it then? Tamrin wondered in reference to Shen's revelation that Shen was the infamous Harbinger of the previous night.

Tamrin had suspected but dismissed the notion of the assumption that his best friend wouldn't hide such a secret from him. But he had.

So rather than hide it, Tamrin chose to invoke the fear of the Harbinger. Unfortunately, somehow, that wasn't enough anymore. Had the Harbinger's reputation grown so large that others actually had tried that tactic to get free?

One couldn't blame people for trying if that was the case, but it sure diluted the effect it should have had coming from Tamrin's mouth. He cursed at the air. Tamrin was afraid something like this would happen if they separated the party. He knew they wouldn't be able to avoid the Raysons on this trek. If not for that netherstack, they would have. But the sense of foreboding he felt told him this was a bad idea.

Shamna's tits, we rolled the cursed five, he thought. *Focus, buddy. Gotta save Jes.*

In an effort to make himself harder to see, Tamrin struck out at torches with his hammer as he passed, sending them toward where he'd first awoken from his unconscious state. Or at least he hoped that was the case. He worried he'd already gotten himself turned around.

He struck the third torch, and it flew almost thirty feet before it landed in a spray of sparks before it went down. He hoped the ploy would work and that the Raysons would behave like most pack animals and run an intercept course rather than track his path.

Tamrin stripped off his furs as he went, leaving little pieces behind. He kept all but the little bakru fur per Shen's request.

He struck one more torch for good measure. When it fell, and the embers floated across the wet ground and were snuffed out, Tamrin reversed course and headed back the way he came, naked all the way to the soles of his feet.

A loud scream, high pitched, sounded in the distance, and Tamrin knew his time was up. The hunters were on the prowl. Tamrin felt a twinge of fear that bordered on paralytic terror from the scream. He sensed the power in it. Had he not heard it before while in his beastly form, it might have caused him to panic this time. Instead, he could recognize the fear and fight it off with relative ease. The scream was answered by several more screams, deeper in the mist and back toward where he'd come.

The mist ebbed and flowed in patches of thick fog intermingled with moments of heightened visibility. He spotted a large tree he'd passed by earlier. As his eyes adjusted to the darkness and shadows began to stand out, he made his way there. He crouched low to the ground, his hammer close to his chest, and reached the thick trunk. He took a moment to hide behind it. He rested his hammer on the ground, afraid he'd react without the stealth necessary to find Jesmir.

Twigs snapped, and wet leaves squished beyond the tree's trunk and drew his attention. Tamrin readied himself and placed his back on the trunk, its rough bark cushioned against his hairy back. From the cadence and volume, he knew it was one of the Raysons approaching quickly. Decades of hunting had honed Tamrin's ability to interpret sound.

The Rayson appeared on his left. Tamrin wasn't prepared for the appearance of the dark skin and pale eyes. But it was dressed exactly like the human form of Raysons he'd seen earlier. Tamrin realized for the first time that the Raysons were shapeshifters. With quiet rage, Tamrin struck.

The creature never stood a chance to react. Tamrin's hands were on the Rayson's mouth and head before it knew the danger. Tamrin snapped the creature's neck with a twist and pulled it close. He eased it onto the ground, grabbed his hammer, and headed farther down his chosen path.

Dark, straight shadows became more frequent, and Tamrin realized he had moved through a denser portion of the trees. He kept low and moved with slow stealth, born of years of practice. He wished he could move as quietly as Shen, but nobody moved without sound.

A twig snapped, and Tamrin froze. To his right, through the trees, a shadow passed before a small circle of light in the mist. The shadow was much closer than the distant torch. Tamrin remained motionless, unwilling to make a sound. The shadow passed toward Tamrin's deception.

Tamrin said a silent prayer to Fildeus in gratitude that the Raysons were not as bright as most societies. Tamrin felt it was because of generational inbreeding and lack of contact with other societies.

Tamrin continued to follow the path he'd laid out for himself. He maintained his proximity to the small circles of light in the fog, their beacons the only point of reference to keep himself near the camp.

He wished he had his periapt.

Another twig snapped behind him in the distance, and Tamrin's heart jumped. Someone found his tracks.

BAD NUTRITION

The mist thinned, revealing more details of the camp hidden within. The home of the Raysons was much larger than Jesmir expected and impoverished. Jesmir marveled at the lack of permanence in the Raysons' lifestyle. Though torch-lined, the paths were barely worn. They crossed each other in an organized pattern that looked freshly laid out. There were no huts or shacks to protect the Raysons from the elements. The only structures were a series of modest lean-tos made from branches over beds made of twigs and leaves–the kind of places attractive to ticks.

Jesmir gazed at the scene before him. There were no signs of children. There was only the noise of bodies moving through the mist that now had receded several yards away.

Uncertain of the best path to find Tamrin, Jesmir ran in the direction he thought the women who'd held him captive ran. Ahead in the thin mist, he noticed a fire where a large cauldron hung, steam rising from the inside. He stopped and inspected the contents of the concoction that brewed over the fire. Various herbs, tree roots, and mushrooms bubbled at the top of the bubbling broth. He looked around for signs of other fires and was surprised to find no other fires like the one before him.

If this is all the stew for the entire population, no wonder they are malnourished, he thought.

Another scream from the mist caused his muscles to lock and his heart to race. His bow fell from his hands as he clasped his ears. The terror induced by the scream was something he couldn't reason himself through. He shook, and the force of the shivers threatened to tear him apart from the inside. The scream died, and Jesmir could breathe again. With shaky hands, he reached down and snatched up his bow.

Jesmir looked once more at the stew and wondered how the Raysons had survived at all with so little.

Tamrin. Find Tamrin, he admonished to himself.

Jesmir once again moved toward the edge of the fog that had now moved farther away. He ran forward, his fear locked in his throat. Jesmir noted how much more he feared the death of Tamrin over his own death, and the realization gave him courage. He chased the receding mists with abandon.

He was only a few feet from the thick fog when he noticed a strangely shaped shadow just inside the swirling barrier. It looked like a table, only taller, almost chest high. Jesmir stepped into the mist and approached the object. He drew within a few feet and choked down a gasp. Before him sat a wooden altar covered in blood. Ropes placed at the corners with slip knots were tied to thick stakes. Jesmir recognized them as restraints.

For humans.

He swallowed hard, his imagination wild with theories. His nerves on edge, he inspected the area and noticed he stood in a bed of strange mushrooms, difficult to discern in the mist. Curious, he knelt down to examine the fungi, and he realized that the altar rested in a bed of mushrooms. The soil around the altar had been tilled, mixed with compost, and, based on the smell, no small amount of feces.

Jesmir winced at the thought and took several steps backward till he no longer stood in the strange garden. He turned to head toward Tamrin when a memory from his studies struck him. He glanced back at the stew, contemplating what he'd seen there, and then knelt back down to inspect the mushrooms.

Bangle's Bane, he thought. *They must not know!*

Jesmir felt like a piece of a puzzle. He had no idea he was working on falling into place. He had to get moving. Tamrin needed to know what he'd found. Maybe they could use it to help the Raysons, and by helping, perhaps the Raysons would set them free.

Wherever Tamrin was, Jesmir needed to be. The prince readied his bow and stepped farther into the blinding mists.

CONFRONTING DEMONS

Tamrin knelt on one knee, his hammer poised, ready for the creature to approach. With an explosion of power, he rose upward and swung the heavy hardwood hammer toward the monster in an uppercut. It slammed into the Rayson's chin, and the dark shadow was knocked backward, its neck broken. Tamrin didn't wait to see if it got up from its injury. Before it landed, the big man sprinted farther through the trees.

The Rayson hit what Tamrin assumed to be the trunk of a tree with a loud crash. Screams echoed from where he'd left his furs. They'd located his trail. It appeared most of the Raysons had done what he expected and ran an intercept course for his perceived location.

The presence of the one he'd just dispatched, however, meant some had tracked him. He cursed quietly to himself for underestimating them. The Raysons seemed to be smarter than they appeared and had taken a dual approach in the hunt. The Raysons wouldn't make that mistake again.

Rapid footsteps drew closer, and he realized they'd figured out where he was. He only hoped they wouldn't figure out where he was headed. At least his ruse bought him precious minutes. Tamrin did his best to track a circle around the camp. He used the shadows of trees as his guide forward and the torches as a meter for his proximity to the camp.

A dark form crouched in the mist ahead, its posture one of loaded readiness. The curved shadow from its hand showed it was a Rayson. It screamed. Tamrin shook off the fear and charged forward. The Rayson leapt in the air, the curve of its blade in an arc downward.

Tamrin wasted no time. He spun from the path of the Rayson and grabbed its ankle mid-leap. Cold once again seized his fingers, and he released his hold, but not before the Rayson's trajectory was disrupted. The black and blue-skinned monster fell to the ground, and with a quiet exhale, Tamrin brought his hammer down atop its head. A sickening thud echoed in the trees, and blood splattered on Tamrin's naked body. The impact made more noise than he intended, and Tamrin sensed the Raysons had located his position. The footsteps in the mist grew quiet.

Tamrin ran his only path, a hasty retreat away from the body. But his pace made too much noise, and the sounds of footsteps, rapid and angry, approached from all sides. Several shadows passed before torchlights. With surprising speed, they closed in on his position. Tamrin stopped and realized he was surrounded. He stepped from the trees and into the mist-covered camp.

To his left, the numbers were fewer. Four shadows approached, each with their curved blades ready. Everywhere else, the shadows of the Raysons blended so that he couldn't count their numbers.

He glanced back at the four. He did not know what direction he faced. He was no longer sure he worked his way toward Jesmir. He only knew that to survive, there was one easier path, but he had to act quickly.

Tamrin surged toward the four darkening shadows that offered his best chance of escape, his hammer already in full swing. The Raysons split apart, but Tamrin was able to target one. The lead Rayson tried to dodge, but Tamrin was too seasoned for the Rayson. He caught the creature in the chest and sent the monster into the lone companion on its right. Both Raysons tumbled to the ground. The other two flanked him and swiped at him with their blades.

Tamrin spun out of the way of the first attack and blocked the second with the hammer's head. The metal struck the wood with a loud thump, and the curved blade stuck in the hardwood. Tamrin twisted the hammer, and the blade was torn from the Rayson's hand.

Tamrin's momentum kept him in constant motion. He never let the hammer come to rest. But his strength wore out. His head still pounded from the lump, and the strenuous activity caused the blood to pump harder. He knew he needed to run, but the Raysons were too close now. He faced the two as he continued to follow through with each swing, twisting his body to keep his eyes on both attackers. The Raysons could see their prey was tiring, and they pressed him farther back into the camp. They rushed together, unafraid. Behind them, another twenty or more shadows came into focus.

His gambit had failed.

He was alone and outnumbered. Jesmir would pay the price. He had no more strength left. He had no chance of survival. He held his hammer, ready for the onslaught. If he had to die, he'd die fighting.

"I'm sorry, Shen," Tamrin whispered into the mist.

SWINGS & ARROWS OF
OUTRAGEOUS FORTUNE

Jesmir crouched low and followed the sounds of chaos and battle, certain he'd pinpointed Tamrin's direction. The mist swirled around him. He moved with haste, his ears focused on the sounds of grunts and crunched twigs. Somewhere in the veil, he heard a thud, heavy and ominous. Several more horrifying screams rang out, the same as before. Once again, Jesmir froze in panic, the involuntary reaction like that of a frightened animal. He tried to fight against the fear, but it consumed him and threatened to drive him mad. He grit his teeth and willed himself to remain still and quiet. If he could hide, maybe these monsters wouldn't find him. Perhaps he could escape.

As before, the scream ended, and the horror subsided. But the fear lingered. His body shook with it.

What the hell am I doing? He thought. *I'm no warrior.*

People like Tamrin and Shen risked their lives every day for people in need. People like Jesmir and his sister. Those men had skills he only dreamed of. Tamrin accessed magic that Jesmir had never been granted access to. Even Jesma, with her relationship to Ezra, had the ability to heal.

Jesmir had nothing but his ability to understand people, his education, and his roguish smile, which made him the most desired bachelor in Teshket. He brought little value to the heat of battle.

Warrior or not, Jesmir thought, *I'm no coward. Fear won't stop me.*

Jesmir resolved himself to the inevitable. If this was how the gods intended him to die, at least he'd die with dignity. No matter how unskilled he was, he refused to give in.

But what about Jesma? he thought.

His heart ached over the decision to leave her. He should never have allowed the party to separate. If he couldn't exercise authority as the Prince of Teshket in matters regarding his own person or that of his sister, when the hell could he? But this wasn't the time to chastise or second guess. What was done was done. He had sufficient enough trouble ahead of him at the moment. He needed Tamrin as much as Tamrin needed him right now.

Besides, without Tamrin, he had no clue where to meet his sister. He'd never been to Rogue's Pointe. He had no idea how to get there. He sure as hell couldn't run around asking strangers for directions.

No. His only choice was to rescue Tamrin or die in the attempt.

Another loud crack sounded in the mist ahead, followed by another thump against the ground. Jesmir wrestled his thoughts into submission and hurried forward. Four dark shadows came into view and took shape. He marveled at how his sight adjusted to the darkness now. Though the mist obscured all details, and the night sky offered little light to penetrate, Jesmir could begin to distinguish the darker shadows with the swirl of wet air. He rushed forward toward a dim, larger shadow amidst the smaller ones.

Jesmir could sense that he approached unseen. From the way they moved, he knew the dark shadows faced the opposite direction of him. Jesmir could separate Tamrin's shadow from the Raysons.

He watched as Tamrin barreled through the line of monsters, his hammer cutting through the mist. Jesmir stood in awe as Tamrin slammed one Rayson into another, and both went down in a heap. His heart caught in his throat as the other two Raysons flanked the giant tracker and attacked in unison. Tamrin successfully dodged one and blocked the other.

Why hasn't he used his magic? Jesmir wondered.

He was about to call out to Tamrin to pray when more creatures emerged from the mist beyond where the man fought for his life. Jesmir observed the line of shadows, an angry mob like the line of an army, prepared to attack Tamrin en masse.

The first arrow flew through the mist without hesitation. Jesmir didn't even remember stretching the bowstring or taking aim. The second arrow followed while the first was still in the air. He reached for the third arrow as the first arrow found its target. The Rayson closest to Tamrin dropped in, and the second fell as the third arrow flew toward the skull of the nearest shadow in the line.

Tamrin turned with surprise, and his heart leapt with relief. Against the backdrop of distant torches, he saw the dark form of Jesmir and watched as more arrows pierced the mist, their aim true. Tamrin rushed to Jesmir as the prince released two more arrows at the dark shadows. Tamrin didn't need to look. He heard the bodies fall and knew the arrows found their marks.

"Boy, am I glad to see you," Tamrin said with a smile.

"Why haven't you changed?" Jesmir cried.

Tamrin pointed at his beard with one hand and prepared to strike the approaching hoard with his hammer in the other. Jesmir realized what Tamrin meant, and his heart sank.

"They took your periapt?" Jesmir said.

"Yes. Just like I imagine they did yours," Tamrin replied.

Jesmir paused and let out a victorious cry. The line of Raysons paused. Jesmir remembered his unanswered prayer. He fired another arrow, and another Rayson fell to the ground. In seconds, they would be too close for his arrows. He reached into his pocket, yanked out the periapt

Tamrin had given him earlier, and slammed it into his protector's giant fist. The Raysons let out another scream, this time many at once.

Jesmir froze again, his hand clasped in Tamrin's. Tamrin, unfazed, recognized the feel of the stone periapt immediately and prayed.

Fildeus answered, and Tamrin's eyes glowed orange. His body once again transformed. The Raysons watched as the mist filled with the massive form of the beast they'd witnessed earlier. Their screams died out, and they stopped their advance less than ten feet from where the pair stood.

Tamrin's transformation took less than a few seconds. He challenged the Raysons with his own scream. The roar echoed through the basin. He stepped to the front of the throng of hunters, intent on his demise. Jesmir launched another arrow at a Rayson on Tamrin's flank.

"Stop!" the leader of the Raysons called with a desperate and frightened voice.

Everyone froze except Tamrin, whose clawed hand was already in full motion. The large spikes of his left hand pierced the eyes of a Rayson. Tamrin removed his hand in a hasty retraction before the cold could once again cause him any discomfort. The body collapsed at his feet. The other Raysons prepared to attack, but the leader stepped forward, and the mist thinned out.

"I said stop," he pleaded and looked up at Tamrin. "You've killed too many of us."

He looked around, saddened by the dwindling numbers of his family.

"You've taken a quarter of my family. This wasn't supposed to happen. We only try to survive. Without your young friend, we have no hope of continuing."

"You left us no choice," Tamrin replied in a deep bellowing tone. "We are not yours to take. I warned you not to do this."

The man looked down at the bodies of his kin, sadness in his eyes. The man closed his eyes, and tears traced a trail in his dirt-lined face. His body shuddered with a heavy sigh.

"We cannot sustain more losses. Even if we beat you, the cost will be too great. We will allow you to leave the Basin. Just don't kill any more of us."

Jesmir stepped forward. "I saw your altar."

"Yes, it is the altar of Quietius. We use it to bring him more followers. We are the last of his people."

"The mushrooms?" Jesmir asked.

"They offer certain psychedelic properties that bring us closer to the Lord of the Final Slumber. We brew it in our stew."

Jesmir felt the pieces fall into place, and he placed a hand on Tamrin's arm.

"They aren't evil," Jesmir said. "Just misguided." He faced the leader of the Raysons. "I've studied at the great universities of Teshket and Rhinestab. One of the many courses I've taken is mycology."

The Rayson leader looked at Jesmir, confused. Jesmir continued.

"The study of mushrooms. Bangle's Bane is known to harm fertility in male offspring when consumed by pregnant mothers. Just one mushroom will cause irreparable harm. Continued consumption will result in the same for grown men."

The man stared at Jesmir as if the prince were speaking in gibberish.

"You are causing your own demise," Jesmir said. "Stop eating the mushrooms."

"But we can't," the man said. "Quietius demands we eat them. He brought them to us. If we don't, he will no longer grant us magic. Without it, we are powerless and will never survive."

Jesmir glanced at Tamrin, who shrugged.

"But if you don't, then you'll forever be infertile," Jesmir replied, dumbfounded. "Why would Quietius ask this of you?"

"Ours is not to question the gods but to do as they request. We are a people of faith. This is what he commands. This is what we do."

"And forcing people to become one of you? Is that part of his command?" Tamrin asked.

"No. It's what we do to survive. To continue to carry on," the leader said.

"Well, I have no intention of allowing you to take either of us," Jesmir said.

Tamrin raised an eyebrow at Jesmir and readied himself for the fight to begin.

"Do you wish to continue this fight then?" Tamrin asked.

"No. I can't lose another member of my family. I wish you both gone from my home," the man said. The other Raysons mumbled amongst themselves, some in dismay. The leader held up his hand to silence them. The camp fell quiet.

"Bring me my gear," Tamrin said.

The man waved at one Rayson to comply.

"And point us to the fastest route to Rogue's Pointe," Tamrin added.

The man pointed to the northeast. The two Raysons returned with Tamrin's gear and furs, and their bodies returned to human shape.

"I hope I never see you again," the leader said, deep sorrow in his tone.

"Pray you don't," Tamrin replied. "For next time I pass through, it will be in the company of the Harbinger. You doubted me before. I'll make a believer of you next time."

A collective gasp worked its way through the Rayson horde. A Rayson stepped forward and returned to human form, Tamrin's gear and furs clutched in his arms. He passed them to Tamrin, who bent down to accept them.

"Go on your way. We will do you no harm," the leader said.

As Tamrin hugged his gear, including all of his furs, to him, he and Jesmir walked through the crowd.

The Rayson woman who had taunted Jesmir earlier stepped close.

"But I must have a baby with those eyes," she lamented.

Tamrin roared in her face, and she stumbled backward. Jesmir shuddered at the thought of her hands on his body. Tamrin stepped forward, and Jesmir followed. The line of Raysons parted way, and the members watched as their prey disappeared into the mist and their hopes of more children faded. The two men, prince and beast, headed in the direction the leader showed, neither daring to look back at the dirty inbred folks known as the Raysons.

PICAROON

The mist departed from them as the Raysons wandered farther into their camp, desperate to put as much distance between the men who'd bested them and what was left of their family as possible. Tamrin released his prayer, and his body returned to his human form. He stopped and dressed himself. His furs were matted with moisture-dripped water as he put them on. When he was finished, Jesmir laughed and said he looked like a wet dog. Tamrin told the prince to shut his trap and strapped his hammer to his back. Then the big man carefully retied his periapt into his beard. When everything was in place. He took a deep breath and exhaled in relief.

With a sheepish and grateful smile, he handed the other periapt back to Jesmir. Jesmir accepted the stone symbol of Fildeus by putting it back in his pocket.

"You aren't going to wear it?" Tamrin asked.

"She ignored me, too. But it's good I had it on me back there."

"Aye," Tamrin said with a smile, "It's good at that. Thank you, Jes. You saved my skin."

Jesmir smiled briefly, but it was short-lived. He knew, deep down, that he'd got lucky. A lot of things could have gone wrong. Men like Tamrin didn't need luck. Men like Jesmir did. It bothered him. Whether of Shamna or just circumstance, Jesmir didn't care which. He just knew in his heart that luck was no way to live.

Jesmir thought about the events of the evening. He wondered how he might recover his life if every turn revealed new dangers. He'd never realized how dangerous the world was—or how ill-prepared he was to face those dangers. Though they'd survived the ordeal, Jesmir's sense of himself as a failure began to weigh on him.

Tamrin clapped him on the shoulder and noticed the blood on the prince's back.

"Hey, Jes," he said. "You're bleeding."

"Yeah, it was the only way to escape the ropes they tied me with."

"We need to get you some healing. That can get infected pretty quickly."

"My sister can take care of me when we get to Rogue's Pointe. You think we'll get there in time?" Jesmir asked.

"Well, our odds improved since we were able to cut through Garrow's Basin. We'll make up time now that we don't have to go around it."

They walked in silence for a few steps before Jesmir changed the subject.

"What do you think about what they said about Quietius? Why wouldn't he want his followers to procreate?" Jesmir asked.

"It's an interesting question, Your Highness. But I don't find the gods like to give many answers. Come, let's find the road to debauchery. I think we've earned it tonight."

Jesmir wasn't satisfied with Tamrin's response, but he knew it wouldn't do any good to continue the conversation. But the idea bothered Jesmir. Something about the idea seemed strange. In a world of temples bent on proselytization, he couldn't understand why one would choose to diminish his followers' ability to increase their numbers. For that matter, he wondered why Quietius wouldn't empower them to improve their living environment. Why did the followers of Quietius live in poverty when most other gods led their followers to prosperity?

Whatever the reason, Jesmir felt compassion for the people he'd just escaped. He thought of the members of the Raysons he'd killed. His mood turned morose, and he was overcome with guilt, though he knew they'd left him with little choice.

Whatever was behind the mystery of Quietius' reasons, Jesmir vowed to uncover them. If he could find answers, maybe he could return to Garrow's Basin one day and help the Raysons. It was the least he could do for killing five of their numbers.

Tamrin, unconcerned with the matters of a god he barely knew, felt a great sense of relief over how they escaped the Raysons. He'd never thought he could survive an encounter with them without Shen at his side. But Prince Jesmir proved more capable than the little guy gave himself credit for. Tamrin vowed to help Jesmir find his personal strength. The prince had a lot of heart, more heart than many warriors twice his age and skill. Tamrin couldn't ignore that. He valued a person's heart over all other things.

It was why he had become close with Shen. Jesmir and Shen shared a lot of common traits that Tamrin valued. With a sideways glance, he smiled at the prince, who once again seemed to be lost in his own head, much the way Shen tended to behave.

Tamrin laughed to himself, happy to be back on the path to Rogue's Pointe. He couldn't relate to the way Shen and Jesmir locked themselves away in their heads. His way was open and free. The big man, true to form, tried to pull Jesmir out of his shell and fell back into stories of the past.

"I ever tell you the story of when Shen and I fought a hundred spiderlyches in one night?" he said to the prince, who walked in somber silence beside him.

Jesmir pushed the negative thoughts down, relieved for the reprieve, and chose instead to listen to the crazy stories Tamrin told of monsters and animals Jesmir had never heard of. He listened for miles as Tamrin regaled him with tales at the side of Fildeus on one of his many Wild Hunts. Jesmir almost laughed out loud when Tamrin said he had the pleasure to speak with the goddess on one such hunt, certain Tamrin made the story up.

They walked and talked until the road into Rogue's Pointe finally appeared.

They'd barely been on the path for a mile when two young men rode in full gallop on horses, each towing an unmanned horse behind. The two men came to a halt before Jesmir and Tamrin.

"Well, if this doesn't look like a beast of a man," the younger of the two said with a smile laced with mirth.

"I'd think twice today, fellas," Tamrin replied. "While I'd love nothing more than to thrash a couple of Picaroons hell-bent on causing me trouble, we are a bit tired, and my temper isn't very long-suffering at the moment."

The two men laughed with heartfelt amusement. Neither threatened the pedestrians before them.

"Well, as much as we'd love to take you on and steal your money, we are in a bit of a hurry. You wouldn't happen to be Master Tamrin, would you?"

"Who's asking?" Tamrin replied.

"I am Kashni, Crown Prince of Ariki Patrin, soon to be King of the Picaroons if Shamna is so willing. This fine man is my cousin, Cristov," Kashni replied, his arm extended to the other rider.

"And why would you be looking for this Master Tamrin?" Tamrin asked.

"We heard that this Master Tamrin was a hell of a lover. I have siblings in dire need of a good bedding. I'm to locate him post haste and bring him to Rogue's Pointe. I'm told he travels with a family friend of a friend of ours. I do hope you are he," Cristov said.

"Who sent you?" Jesmir asked.

"Well, that information will cost you," Kashni said. "But as you are family, we shall give you a discount. Give us a dance!"

"Son of a bitch," Tamrin mumbled. "Come on," he said to Jesmir. "I know who sent these two."

"Aha! You are master, Tamrin! D'aonar sends his regards, and Father sends horses. We are to escort you to Rogue's Pointe with haste."

"D'aonar?" Jesmir asked.

Tamrin flicked his wrists in a motion to show blades like Shen used. Jesmir nodded in understanding. Raised a hand in acquiescence to the pair on horseback.

"Take us to D'aonar…and your horny siblings," Tamrin said with a smirk.

"Oh, if you aren't friends of our friend, then no one is!" Kashni said with a perfect grin.

Tamrin and Jesmir each mounted one of the spare horses and Jesmir turned his on the road to face north.

"I don't suppose we could take it easy riding back?" Tamrin asked.

"Hell no," Jesmir said and spurred his horse into a full gallop, eager to get away from Garrow's Basin and reach his sister.

"Son of a bitch," Tamrin said.

He spurred his horse on and did his best to keep up. He reminded himself to have words with Shen when he saw him next. Tamrin hated to ride horseback, well-trained Picaroon horse or not.

Cristov and Kashni laughed and hollered as they gave chase after the two men they'd been sent to find, eager to get back to the lively festivities that awaited at Rogue's Pointe.

THE END

A NOTE FROM THE AUTHOR

Much of the World Of Conishant is fleshed out. In order to move THE GOD KILLERS trilogy along, it had to be. But there are still many holes and gaps to fill as the story of Shen, Tamrin, Jesma, and Jesmir unfolds.

Those who have read and finished THE GROWING DARKNESS seem to love the characters and are genuinely invested in what happens to them. Many of you reached out, hungry for more from the adventure, ready to dive in and see where this will all lead. I've been overwhelmed by the response of so many of your reactions to these characters that I've grown to love.

When I chose to write THE GOD KILLERS trilogy in the first person, it was an easy choice. The intent was always to immerse the reader in the torment of Shen's mind. This is mainly because the overall themes the story is designed to convey require such storytelling methods. Shen's battles with self-doubt, fear of abandonment, insecurity, fear of inadequacy, and the mental anguish that comes from his darker thoughts work only through the first-person narrative.

An unfortunate side effect of this choice is that readers' perspectives of the other characters outside of Shen's point of view are hard to illustrate. Truthfully, that was the hardest aspect of writing THE GROWING DARKNESS.

I've grown to love Tam, Jez, and Jes as much as I do Shen. I know them as intimately as I do the lovably broken protagonist of the Conishant. Through reviews and social media, many of you have expressed the desire to know them as well. I know several fans who love Tamrin or Jesmir as their favorite characters.

I'm a big fan of novellas. Few things thrill me more than when a favored author offers a new perspective or side story of a world I've already fallen in love with. I love world-additive mini-stories that can be read in an afternoon by the pool or lazily on the couch or on the cliffs during a vacation in Rhode Island while sitting in an Adirondack chair with an Old Fashioned made from my favorite bourbon.

It has always been my intention to find some way to relay the story of what happened in Garrow's Basin.

Originally written as a short story of less than 9,000 words, the story of what happened on the side quest on which I sent Tamrin and Jesmir seemed flat. It had no purpose that drove any portion of the overarching story forward.

In short, it was a self-indulgent filler with no heart—the opposite of the characters it was meant to convey who are full of heart.

It was Amanda Miller (@the_trashy_reader) who approached me on Instagram with the demand that I give everyone more on "Tam-Tam," as she so lovingly calls Tamrin, and "Jes," whom she may or may not have inside information on. Such were Amanda's thoughts on the matter that I felt "Garrow's Basin" deserved better treatment than just a short story.

You were right, Amanda!

Thanks to Amanda, I discovered, to my sincerest pleasure, that readers want to know these supporting characters on a deeper level. "Garrow's Basin" presented an opportunity to tell a story that not only revealed the hearts of Tamrin and Jesmir but also allowed you to ride with them on an essential point of their growth journey. I hope, as always, that you enjoyed this story as much as I enjoyed writing it.

And, if you do enjoy this story, and happen to join the Discord or follow along on Instagram, reach out to Amanda and thank her. This never would have happened had she not been so persuasive.

ACKNOWLEDGEMENTS

Foremost and always, to Jill, my amazing, beautiful, intelligent, opinionated, outspoken, and kind wife. Your spirit, compassion, and joy are the beacon that keeps me moving forward. If not for your honesty, encouragement, and support, I'd never have found the courage to do this. I love you more than words can express, and I show it half as much as I should, yet you stand with me, an eternal life partner. It's with great joy and laughter that we walk this life together, and I'm all the better for it. I love you more today than I did yesterday. You're my favorite person.

To my editors at Writer's Journey Services, Laura Thompson and RB Michaels, I extend my eternal gratitude. You two challenge every word I write, and I'm grateful for that. As always, I kick and scream at you when you tell me something needs to be changed. I appreciate your guidance and your shoves. Every round of edits makes these books and stories better.

To my illustrator, Serena Dunlap, how weird it is that you came to my book launch for the Growing Darkness as a reader, and now we work together? I appreciate you! Thank you for the time and effort you put into creating the illustrations throughout this novella. We wanted a specific style and feel to them, and you nailed it.

To Amanda Miller and Andrea Uvanni, my beta readers, street team coordinators, and all-around champions. "Delegate, Sean!" echoes in my head 100 times a day. Your unhinged love for the characters, suggestions on story arcs, and constant shoutouts to the world about THE GOD KILLERS series has been the most rewarding part of publishing. Thanks for putting up with my shenanigans, absent-mindedness, disorganized plans, and missteps along the way! (Amanda, I hope GARROW'S BASIN gave you what you asked for!)

To CITY OF ASYLUM BOOKSTORE and the staff there—especially Phoenix Tefel. You've been amazing. The support, love, and excitement you bring to every event has been nothing short of overwhelming. Thank you for the effort, their discussions, and for tolerating my chattiness. The support you've given on this journey continues to fill my heart with joy. Thank you for everything. The launch party for THE GROWING DARKNESS was an amazing success and that wouldn't have happened without you and the amazing staff!

To my amazing fellow indie authors who I've had the extremely great fortune to become friends with: Caytlyn Brooke, Arlo Z Graves, Atlas Creed, and Marc Avery. You all make my day! It is with great pleasure that I share the trenches of indie authorship with you. I also added a link to your works at the end of this book. You are all very talented writers, and I only hope I make you proud!

Finally, to every reader and follower on Instagram, Threads, TikTok, Discord: From the depths of my soul, thank you for reading. Ultimately, it's you that drives the success of THE GOD KILLERS. If you didn't read, review, and tell your friends about this story, it would just collect dust. I hope you continue to read and enjoy the wild rides to come!

All the best to everyone!

<u>Check Out Works From these Amazing Indie Authors</u>

Caytlyn Brooke—The Skyglass Duology
https://caytlynbrooke.wixsite.com/booksbycaytlyn

Arlo Z Grave—Black Rose
https://www.arlozgraves.com/

Atlas Creed—Children of Arcanum Series
https://www.atlascreedauthor.com/

Marc Avery—Discipline
https://iammarcavery.com/

EXCERPT FROM THE UPCOMING NOVEL

RUBY RAGE:
FROM THE CASE FILES OF MILES WARD

Cleveland National Forest
Orange County, CA
April 18th, 1944

The tiny whimpers of twelve-year-old Katy McCoy haunted Miles as he struggled to shake off the trauma of what he'd just witnessed. Her small voice, frail and frightened, lingered like the screams of his fellow Marines in the Pacific. The sound of her cries overshadowed the memory of the gunshots that killed her abductor.

But not of the gunshot that killed her.

He got the bad guy. But he couldn't save the child.

Miles knew he'd never recover from the choice he made. There was little he could do ease young Katy's suffering. Survival was not an option for the child he'd spent weeks trying to find. A life of suffering was all that remained, her injuries too extensive.

Miles wanted to run to the car and call out on the radio for help, but that would have required him to leave the poor child alone in that place. She would have died before he returned, and she would have done so alone.

He couldn't let that happen. Miles understood what Katy did not. Katy's fate was sealed long before he arrived on the scene. Miles would have to live with the fact that he was too late, that he wasn't good enough to get to her in time. It took too long to find the old house in the middle of the forest.

If I'd only been faster.

Instead, he held young Katy's shattered and broken body close as she cried in pain. He whispered to her that everything would be okay—that a better place waited for her—even though, in his heart, he believed no such place existed. Miles held her tiny head, her life's blood coating him, as she took her last breath in his lap. He screamed until his voice was lost, unable to comprehend the severity of his failure.

His last words to her were that her parents loved her.

She died in his arms. But at least she didn't die alone.

Miles' blood-stained hands shook, the adrenaline long since receded. The reality of his experience took hold of his mind. His ears still rang from the successive concussions that echoed through the house as he'd emptied his Colt M1911A1 into the monster that tortured and murdered the young girl. Miles' began to shake with cold sweats and rage.

Steady and decisive in action, Miles always fell apart in the aftermath. Inevitably, his confidence gave way to second guesses, regrets, and "shoulda-couldas". He knew he'd soon crash against the rocks of his own inner doubts. An emotional tsunami was imminent. Guilt, fear, and second guessing threatened to pull him under water as he fought in panicked desperation to cling to a small portion of his sanity.

Things he thought he could avoid now stared him in the face. The genetic erosion of his sanity had begun; his perceptions of the world skewed by the same ailments passed along through his mother's bloodline. Reason said that what he saw wasn't possible. But he had witnessed the impossible. Now the doubt was gone.

He'd finally gone insane. Reality and fantasy mingled and created images that seemed too real to be denied. He couldn't deny their validity at the time.

Now, in the aftermath, the steady assuredness with which he'd just acted appeared less certain.

He finally crashed.

Hard.

Across the overgrown lawn, his partner, Thom, spoke with Captain Samuels in hushed tones. A kaleidoscope of blue and red lights bathed the surrounding forest and the dilapidated Queen Anne Victorian home in bright strobing colors. The headlights from the coroner's meat wagon illuminated the house, dark shadows of overgrown vines the only evidence of the spooky ghosts inside.

If only Thom had finished his part of the search in Hollywood Hills sooner, he could have been there to witness what Miles saw. But he didn't. His long-time partner arrived too late.

Just like Miles arrived too late to save Katy McCoy.

Thom glanced over to his partner and friend who leaned, slumped, against his 1940 Ford Standard Coupe.

Thom was in a pickle. He'd heard the words come out of Miles' mouth, words so unbelievable that he was sure Miles' time was up. If he didn't believe Miles' story, there was little chance Captain Samuels would. They most certainly would send Miles to the looney bin.

The tale was too fantastical. Worse yet, everybody knew Miles' family history of psychotic breaks that stretched back generations. Miles' tale was ghost story, a tale used to scare children at campfires. The stuff of monsters and magic—of boogey-men.

"Have him checked out by psych," Captain Samuels said, equal parts concern and command.

"Yes, sir," Thom said. He made his way over to Miles who still leaned against the car door, head bowed, arms crossed.

"Hey ace, how you holding up?" Thom asked.

Miles extinguished a cigarette on the heal of his boot.

"I don't understand. I know what I saw. It's not what you think, Thom."

Thom lowered his voice, afraid they'd be overheard.

"I know what you believe you saw, but I'm telling you, there's no evidence to back the claim." Thom sighed. "Let it go. You got the guy. He was just a whacko who did a horrible thing," Thom said.

Miles shook his head, defiant.

"Hey, pal. That asshole needed put down and you did it. But he is, or was, as human as you and me. That's all."

"I'm telling you," Miles said through clenched teeth, "I know what I saw."

"Okay. But listen, if you continue with this—" Thom stopped. He whispered, "Partner, you sound crazy."

The uncertainty in Miles' eyes broke Thom's heart. He knew then, there was no coming back. His friend had fallen to insanity. Thom looked back at the gurney coming from the house.

"C'mere. Come look at the body. Tell me what you see."

Thom put his hand around Miles' shoulder. Miles stood up and looked at Thom, unsure. Thom guided Miles to where the forensics team loaded the perpetrator's body into the coroner's wagon.

"Hold up," Thom said.

The coroner complied, his cigarette dangling loose in his lips.

Miles was terrified to look. He feared Thom was right. No matter how crazy it was, he needed to know the truth. Miles hoped to find that what he saw inside the house was not all in his head. He couldn't shake the image: the eyes, the scales, the oppressive darkness, the claws. He'd already replayed it several time. He saw what he saw. And he knew it was real.

But what if he was wrong?

Thom reached over and pulled the sheet off the body. Miles heart sank and the impending doom of his fate settled in. Instead of a monster, he stared at the body of an elderly man, his face practically unrecognizable from the bullet damage. One hand had a hole in it with a finger blown off.

"Look, Miles, it's just a man. A man you pumped five slugs into."

Miles resisted the truth at first, but it was just as Thom said—no scales, no elongated limbs, no tail.

The man's head had been obliterated by several rounds of .45 caliber bullets. But what remained told the tale. The 'creature' he killed was nothing but a regular old man.

What is going on?, Miles thought.

"Hell is. All of it," the voice said. *"That's why I told you to kill them both."*

Miles shook his head violently.

Thom put a hand on his Miles' shoulder.

"Buddy, you gotta calm down. You've got bigger issues," Thom said.

A second gurney rolled out with the body of Kay McCoy. Thom and Miles watched as they loaded her into the other hearse. Miles heart ached at his failure.

"Tell me again, why did you shoot Katy McCoy?"

Miles stared at Thom unable to speak.